THE
HEADMASTER'S
DILEMMA

Books by Louis Auchincloss

Fiction

The Indifferent Children
The Injustice Collectors
Sybil
A Law for the Lion
The Romantic Egoists
The Great World and Timothy Colt
Venus in Sparta
Pursuit of the Prodigal
The House of Five Talents
Portrait in Brownstone
Powers of Attorney
The Rector of Justin
The Embezzler
Tales of Manhattan
A World of Profit
Second Chance
I Come As a Thief
The Partners
The Winthrop Covenant
The Dark Lady
The Country Cousin
The House of the Prophet
The Cat and the King
Watchfires
Narcissa and Other Fables
Exit Lady Masham
The Book Class
Honorable Men
Diary of a Yuppie
Skinny Island
The Golden Calves
Fellow Passengers
The Lady of Situations

False Gods
Three Lives: Tales of Yesteryear
The Collected Stories of Louis Auchincloss
The Education of Oscar Fairfax
The Atonement and Other Stories
The Anniversary and Other Stories
Her Infinite Variety
Manhattan Monologues
The Scarlet Letters
East Side Story
The Young Apollo and Other Stories
The Friend of Women and Other Stories
The Headmaster's Dilemma

Nonfiction

Reflections of a Jacobite
Pioneers and Caretakers
Motiveless Malignity
Edith Wharton
Richelieu
A Writer's Capital
Reading Henry James
Life, Law and Letters
Persons of Consequence:
Queen Victoria and Her Circle
False Dawn: Women in the
Age of the Sun King
The Vanderbilt Era
Love Without Wings
The Style's the Man
La Gloire: The Roman Empire
of Corneille and Racine
The Man Behind the Book
Theodore Roosevelt
Woodrow Wilson
Writers and Personality

The
Headmaster's
Dilemma

Louis Auchincloss

Houghton Mifflin Company

BOSTON   NEW YORK

2007

For information about permission to reproduce selections from
this book, write to Permissions, Houghton Mifflin Company,
215 Park Avenue South, New York, New York 10003.

Visit our Web site: www.houghtonmifflinbooks.com.

Library of Congress Cataloging-in-Publication Data
Auchincloss, Louis.
The headmaster's dilemma / Louis Auchincloss.
p. cm.
ISBN-13: 978-0-618-88342-4
ISBN-10: 0-618-88342-8
1. School principals—Fiction. 2. Preparatory schools—Fiction.
3. New England—Fiction. 4. Psychological fiction. I. Title.
PS3501.U25H43 2007
813'.54—dc22   2007008522

Book design by Anne Chalmers
Typefaces: Janson Text, Arabesque Ornament MT

Printed in the United States of America

QUM 10 9 8 7 6 5 4 3 2 1

To my friend and editor,
JANE ROSENMAN

THE
HEADMASTER'S
DILEMMA

1

MICHAEL SAYRE thought afterward that it had all started on an early spring afternoon in 1975 when he and Ione and Donald Spencer were sitting in the small rose garden behind the headmaster's house having coffee after Sunday lunch. They had not eaten in the big school dining room at the main table because Donald Spencer, chairman of the trustees, had only limited time for what he had termed an important visit and had requested a meeting alone with the headmaster and his wife.

The residence that rose above them was a charming old New England manor house, and the great boarding school of which it was the center, to match it, had been tastefully conceived as a colonial village of sober and regular white house fronts grouped about a shimmering oblong lawn studded with elms and dominated at one end by the chapel, a chaste meeting house with a tall spire. As the institution had grown and expanded through the decades, other and larger buildings had been added and playing fields lain out, but these had been sufficiently distanced from the original village atmosphere of plain living and high thinking evoked by the school founder in the 1880s. Averhill, for all its four hundred students and great modern reputation, was still considered by many of its alumni and parents as a stalwart fortress against the creeping vulgarity of the day.

And so Michael liked to think of it. He had been headmaster for three years now, appointed as a result of the successful efforts of younger members of the board to convince the others that a leader was needed to make some adaptations to the exigencies of change in educational thinking. And he had already achieved some of these: girls had just been admitted; the limits of the courses widened. He had come to Averhill with a considerable reputation as a liberal; he had been the admired editor of a popular radical newspaper and a nationally known protester of the war in Vietnam, and although some of the more conservative of the school trustees had gagged at his appointment, the general feeling was that if change had to come it had better come through one of their own. Michael himself was a graduate of the school where he had had a brilliant record, and he was supposed to have a deep concern for the original ideals of the institution. It also didn't hurt that he was possessed of striking good looks and had a beautiful, charming wife.

Yet what did all this avail to alleviate the disgust that he felt at what Donald Spencer was now proposing? And the worst of it was that not a single item in the chairman's grandiose scheme was in the least objectionable. It was the case of the whole being greater than the sum of its parts. Much greater.

What Spencer was offering was simply a major addition to the school plant, the cost of which would be provided by his own fortune and those of his wealthy partners and friends. There would be a huge new gymnasium with every conceivable modern appliance, a hockey rink, a nine-hole golf course, a ski run, a swimming pool, new tennis and squash courts, and a small theatre for movies and amateur dramatics. All of these structures would be outside the present campus, but they would double its area and to some extent dwarf the existing buildings.

Spencer saw no objection to this.

"People coming to the school for the first time would not be put off by its note of old-fashioned quaintness. They would recognize at once that they were visiting a thoroughly up-to-date institution with every modern improvement. They would see right away that they were dealing with a school that could rival Andover and Exeter in every sport that can be played!"

An acute observer might have deduced from the different appearances of the headmaster and his chairman the difference in their points of view. They were the same age, forty, and had been formmates at Averhill. Michael was tall, well made, and muscularly coordinated, with a serene pale countenance, a high noble brow, wide-apart calmly gazing blue eyes, and thick long auburn hair. Women were apt to call him beautiful. Spencer was short and plump, with an egg-shaped balding head and suspicious yellow-green eyes. The two were generally supposed to have been on friendly terms, even as schoolboys, and their families had enjoyed cordial relations, yet both had always known, without admitting it to each other or to anyone else, that a mutual dislike and mistrust lay fatally between them.

Donald had expressed no opposition when a unanimous vote of the trustees had invited Michael to take up his present position. He had voiced his objections privately to some of the older board members, but when he had seen that the battle was lost he had gone along with their desire to appear wholly agreed to the alumni. It was his habit, anyway, to conceal dissent so long as dissent served no purpose of his own. He had other ways of implementing his designs. As a boy at Averhill he had proved a rare example of the power of shrewdness over muscle. A poor athlete himself and with unprepossessing looks, he had yet known how to burrow his way into the confidence of the form leaders both by flattering their prowess on the playing field and at the same time letting it be slyly known that his gimlet eye had uncovered their vulnerable spots. He was also skilled at uniting a crowd against a selected opponent by the adroit use of prejudice, thus gaining for himself the reputation of a cleansing authority. The boys had respected him and feared his bitter and wounding tongue.

He had done well enough at Averhill and later at Harvard, but there was always an air about him that he was waiting, biding his time. His real success came after he joined the staff of his father's great Wall Street bank and rapidly achieved a position and a fortune that made the distinguished paternal career seem small in comparison. He took over the mergers and acquisitions department and eventually carved it into a separate company that became famous for its toughness and ruthlessness even in that tough and ruthless field. If the ever-triumphant Donald shed a tear over the destruction of fine old businesses or the widespread loss of jobs, he must have shed it very privately.

It was the envy in Donald's yellow-green eyes, an envy never expressed by his politic lips, that had first alerted Michael, even as a schoolboy, to the awareness that there were aspects of his own personality that might arouse this feeling in others. He had learned that modesty and even humility were the proper companions of self-respect from his father, the eminent and beloved professor of philosophy at Columbia, and had never regarded his own natural gifts as particularly special or given to him for any purpose other than to make the world a tiny bit better. It was hardly his fault that the kind of social success that he so effortlessly attained was precisely the kind that Donald so signally lacked and desperately wanted. Boys, and girls, too, loved Michael. They put up with Donald. One was the innermost of the "ins"; the other would always be on the circumference.

Donald's hostility had waxed with years. The alumni and older faculty members of the school might respect or even revere their famous (or infamous?) chairman for his huge gifts to Averhill, but most of the students (despite their often conservative Republican parents) and virtually all the younger teachers applauded the courageous liberalism of the popular headmaster. Donald knew it was said that he had to buy the approval of his peers; on Michael this approval seemed to rain down from heaven.

"When are you planning to submit this project to the board, Donald?" Michael asked, placing a blueprint on the coffee table before them.

"Just as soon as you okay it. You don't expect any opposition from that quarter, do you?"

"You mean, do I think they'll look this gift horse in the mouth? Never. They'll be dazzled."

A pause followed that Donald interrupted in a somewhat sharper tone. "What about you, Mike? You're with me, are you not?"

Michael was silent, but after some moments he nodded slowly, very slowly, several times. Donald looked at Ione, as if she might give him the answer.

"When Michael nods that way, Donald, it doesn't mean he's agreeing with you. It means he's thinking."

"I'm thinking of what this means to the school, Donald. Not just in terms of improved athletic facilities. But in what it may do to the image of Averhill."

"What can it do but improve it?"

"Aren't you a little begging the question? You know, of course, that in these days the choice of a boarding school has largely passed out of the hands of parents. It's the kids who now make the decisions. Every spring they take off on what they call the school tour, and the poor parents must drive them patiently all over New England to inspect St. Paul's, or Taft, or Hotchkiss, or Choate, or whatever. The day when a Groton grad registered his son on birth for admission to the school he then *had* to attend is long past."

"It's passed for some," Donald retorted, a sneer in his tone. "It hasn't passed for me. When my son Sam asked me when we were to take the 'school tour,' I said, 'Right now, if you like.' At my bidding and to his astonishment we put on our hats and coats and walked up Park Avenue to Eighty-eighth Street where I pointed to a building. 'But, Dad, that's the Robert Wagner High School!' he protested. 'Precisely,' I told him, 'and that's where you're going if you don't go to Averhill.' And hasn't he done well here?"

"Very well indeed. But there aren't many fathers as forceful as you, Don. Ask any of his formmates who made the decision to come to Averhill."

"Well, what's that to me so long as they made the right choice?"

"Because students don't always make it. It's not their fault. How can they have the right criteria at thirteen or fourteen to tell a first-rate school from a second- or even a third-rate one? Naturally, they're going to be impressed by appearances: big gyms, shiny classrooms, well-mown lawns, everything spic and span. What do they know of the quality of teaching or the preparation for a serious mission in life? Those things don't show. Of course, they'll be dazzled by your proposed additions."

"Well, I'll be damned if I see anything wrong with that!

Who cares why they come so long as they come? And I'll tell you something else, my friend. The grander the plant, the easier your future fundraising. The rich like to put their money where other rich have put theirs."

"You mean charity tends to go where it is least needed?"

"That's a cynical way of putting it. I'd rather say that charity prefers success to failure. It helps those who help themselves. We're competing for kids in an area where the kids make the decision. Obviously we have to give them what they want."

"Which means, I take it," Michael commented in a graver tone, "that we have to offer the rich students all the luxuries they have at home. Which costs more and more, so that tuition must rise to pay for each new embellishment. Won't we reach a point where we will have to confine our student body to the *Forbes* list of America's wealthiest?"

"You have your scholarships."

"Yes, but not that many. And there are plenty of parents already who hesitate to send their children to schools where they will rub shoulders with kids whose families have yachts and private jets and who are constantly talking about them."

"Maybe that will whet their ambition to get ahead in a commercial society. Is that such a bad thing? You talk about the *Forbes* list as if it were a catalogue of America's most wanted. But those men are the leaders of our society. It should be our privilege to educate their offspring!"

"You might have more of a point, my dear Donald, if your tycoons could bequeath their brains as well as their money to their progeny. But that, except in your own admirable case, is not often the situation."

"Oh, I know your passion to fill Averhill with the smartest students. But have you ever stopped to think that they're just the ones who don't need Averhill? Getting between a really bright kid and a library or laboratory is like getting between a hippo and the water. They educate themselves! The glory of the private school is something we can't boast about. It's what we can do with the dumbbells."

Michael chose not to reply to this. It was a point that had much troubled him. The real danger of men like Donald was not when they were wrong but when they were right. However, the latter's next remark put him clearly in the wrong.

"And while we're on that subject, Mike, I might observe that I view with some concern the distinct increase of Jewish and Oriental boys in the school since you took over. It's all very well to have some, but there comes a point where you're changing the fundamental character of the institution."

"How many is some?"

"Oh, you can't reduce these things to an exact number. You have to use your discretion, of course."

"And if I have none?" Michael sighed. "We've come a long way from Socrates who needed nothing but a courtyard and a few questions. I don't suppose he worried about the ethnic origin of those he taught."

"Don't you believe it!" Donald exclaimed with a rude chuckle. "He'd have kicked out a Persian!"

Ione now entered the discussion by asking Donald about

the possibility of creating an art gallery for the school where they could mount visiting shows or even start a permanent collection of their own. It was a favorite project of hers, and Donald showed a mild interest in it. Anything interested him, Michael reflected sourly, if it contained the opportunity of putting his name on it in capital letters. He let them talk, dropping out of the conversation, and letting his eyes drift over the playing fields to the blue-black line of the awakening forest.

He was wondering, as he so often found himself doing, if he had been right in taking his present job. It was not a throbbing worry; he was too used to it for that. It was a soft, constant, sometimes even oddly relaxing worry. He had no idea of making a break with his commitment. He had undertaken a task, and he would certainly stick to it. But he was quite able now to contemplate the possibility that he might fail. As the voices of his wife and his chairman jangled in his ear, he could almost fancy her as Eve and him as the serpent in the garden.

But the idea was ridiculous. He had to get away from Donald. Impatiently he arose.

"I'll study these plans tonight, Don, and I'll call you the first thing on Monday. I just can't discuss it further today — I'm sorry. Please forgive me, but I've got to go for a stroll."

As he strode quickly across the empty playing fields toward the blessedly solitary woods, he tried to be fair in his mind to the chairman of the board. After all, even allowing for his egotism, wasn't there some element of generosity in

the throwing of his millions at the school? That many phi-
lanthropists sought personal glory from their bounty did not
mean that nobler motives were total strangers to them. And
shouldn't one pity Donald for the obvious fact that his wealth
had failed to make him happy? How could it when he had always had it? And wasn't his wife an alcoholic? Didn't people
say that she regretted having married him for his money?
And hadn't he suffered at school from a cruel nickname derived from the fact that he had been endowed, at least in his
early teens, with a smaller than usual penis?

At this last thought Michael pulled himself up to shudder
in disgust at the ways of the world. Did history have to be
made out of the resentments of physically underprivileged
great men? Had millions had to die because Napoleon was
stubby and Kaiser Wilhelm had a withered arm and Car-
dinal Richelieu hemorrhoids? Had hundreds of Americans
been thrown out of work and fine old businesses wrecked
because of the late development of Donald Spencer's private
parts? With a weary sigh he turned his steps back toward the
school.

Who was he, after all, to think he could change the world?
What would it gain him to stand between Donald and the
rip tide of his millions? Did he think for a minute that the
board would back him? Did he not know that they would
tear down the chairman's pants and place their lips devoutly
on his fat exposed rear end?

As he approached the headmaster's house he saw that
Donald had left and that Ione was sitting alone at the cof-

fee table idly examining a blueprint. The temperature had dropped and she had put on a striking red sweater that went well with her gold necklace and large gold bracelets. He recalled that she had said that only gold could be worn with sweaters. Her tan hair was also gold-tinted, but the hardness suggested by the shining metal was softened by her beauty. Michael reflected as always that he could get through anything with her behind him.

"You look exhausted, my love," she said as he came up. "You should really have a drink or a vitamin pill before any meeting with dear Donald."

He slumped into the chair beside her. "Oh, he'll have his vulgar sports plaza, I've faced that. There's no fighting his big bucks."

"Yes, but you can moderate them. I've been going over the plans. They can be cut down. The new buildings can be scattered. The whole thing can be spread out and muted."

"But he'd never stand for it, darling. He's got his great architect. The whole thing's a must. It's what he calls a work of art. You can't fiddle with works of art."

"The board may not see it that way."

"Ione, you're dreaming! They'll gobble it up."

"You have friends on the board. More than you think."

"But not enough for a battle like this."

She suddenly stood up, as if to make a great point. "And you have the ace of trumps up your sleeve! You can threaten to resign!"

He too jumped up, but in astonishment. "And if they accept my resignation?"

"Then we'll go! There are plenty of other places that will want you. Do you think, my darling, that I haven't known how often you've been wondering if Averhill is really the right place for you? Or if any New England boarding school is the right place for you?"

He gazed at her in admiration. "Darling, what's got into you?"

2

WHAT INDEED had got into Ione?

From childhood, she had been a deeply serious girl, eager to find the right place for herself in a confusing society and often wondering if such a thing as a right place existed. At Barnard College she had joined the ranks of the majority of the girls in her class who believed that women should keep their maiden names after marriage, have full-time jobs even while raising a family, hold liberal political views, and prefer casual dress to haute couture. The great thing in life was to be natural. The great thing to be avoided was something called fancy pants.

The trouble was that her mother, whose only child she was, seemed the very opposite of much of this. In many ways indeed her parents appeared the essence of fancy pants. And yet they were a brilliantly successful couple; they were even, at least in Manhattan, almost famous. Her father, Ira Fletcher, sleek, slim, ebony-haired, and elegant, was the highly reputed designer of women's wear, and Diane, her mother, the graceful grande dame of urban chic, was the editor of the popular fashion magazine *Style*. Photographs of the couple in splendid evening attire appeared so often in newspaper accounts of Gotham revelry and charity balls that friends made health inquiries if their images were missing for a couple of weeks. Yet for all of this their manners were open and kind; they exuded a charm that won them hearts wherever they went.

Ione's particular difficulty, when she came of college age, was that she couldn't fault them. They both took what had to be a sincere interest in her studies, in her amusements, in her boyfriends, even in her would-be rebellious resistance to their interest in her. They included her in their parties well before her eighteenth year; they apparently saw no reason why she should not fit snugly into their world. They simply did every-thing right—shouldn't that be enough? But wasn't something missing in her mother's delicate peck of a kiss on her cheek, in her father's gentle pat on her back, something like the bear hug she had seen her friends' parents give their offspring? Did she dare to compare the manicured lives of Ira and Diane to a finely produced and expertly acted parlor comedy?

She had no occasion to discuss these doubts with her friends because, without exception, they were all, even the most liberal minded, dazzled by her parents, who greeted them with invariable charm and warmth. But as Ione's grad-uation approached, she began to feel the absolute necessity of a candid discussion with her mother as to her future ca-reer. They *had* to talk frankly, at least once.

She had no sooner started on this than Diane interrupted

to assure her there would always be an opening on the staff of *Style*.

"Oh, no, no, that's not my idea of a career at all!" Ione exclaimed, seizing on this with a kind of desperation to introduce the real topic. "I have in mind something totally different!"

"You sound as if *Style* were beneath you," Diane replied with a mildly reproachful smile.

"Oh, it's not that, Mummy. It's not that really. *Style*'s all very well for those that like it. It's just that . . . well, I'd like to be more in the real world."

"And you think *Style* isn't real?"

"Well, it's not grubby. If that's what I mean."

"You're looking for something grubby? How singular."

"I was thinking of law school."

"Well, I guess that's grubby enough for anyone." Diane paused now to consider this new option. Oh, she was always ready to consider things! "Actually, women are beginning to make great strides in the law. They say Betty Stackpole has made a fortune in divorce cases, and I hear she's going to represent Ted Saunders in his wife's bigamy suit. That should net her a walloping fee."

"Oh, I don't think I'd go in for domestic relations. I'd want a wider field than that. Divorce lawyers make dirty waters dirtier. I'd want something more in the public interest."

"Well, so long as you don't spit at money, my dear. You'll find it can come in very handy. But talk to your father about this. He's had more experience with lawyers than I have. He won a big suit last year against some crazy shop that claimed he'd stolen a design. *That* was grubby enough for anyone."

Ione decided that she would discuss it with Ira that very night, and when he came home he promised that he would go into it with her at dinner, which, for once, they were all three to have alone. But at the last moment the table in the elegant Pompeian dining room had to be reset for four because Ray Adla, the great ballet star, had asked himself suddenly to the meal on the pretext of discussing with Ira the offer from a French ballet company that he had just received.

Adla had been a protégé of the Fletchers ever since his humble and impecunious start, and his subsequent fame had not tempered his gratitude. He consulted them in everything, eagerly and submissively. Ione reflected bitterly, as the evening droned on until bedtime, with her father never seeming to notice that he had promised her an important meeting, that Adla was like the son he had never had.

And then a nasty thought struck her, the fruit, no doubt, of her suddenly aroused jealousy. She had been having some sad talks recently with a Barnard friend who was distraught over her discovery that her beau and lover was finding greater diversion with a member of his own sex. She took note now of the peculiar warmth of her father's treatment of his ballet star. Was it really paternal? Wasn't it something more cherishing? Even more carnal?

The young man was certainly lovely to look at. His every motion was gracefully true to his profession. And his reputation in love, as Ione and his fans well knew, was notoriously bisexual. This, of course, was common in the world of ballet and hardly to be commented on. But what Ione was coldly observing from across the room was not the dancer but her father. He was totally taken with his guest; Ione and her mother for the moment had ceased to exist.

He did, however, find the time to discuss with his daughter at breakfast the next morning her desire to go to law school, but she could not but compare the seemingly perfunctory speed at which he approved her plan with the rapt attention he had given to Adla's problem the night before. Still, his assent and support served to quell her mother's doubts, and Ione found herself enrolled the following fall in New York University Law School, and deriving even greater satisfaction from her courses than she had anticipated. She particularly liked contracts, where she sat by and soon made something of a pal of a sandy, tousled, and tense young man called Tom Murphy who was a deeply devoted student and obviously the type destined to make the law review. He came of a very different background from Ione's — his father was a police detective — but he responded to her friendly overtures and was soon helping her to analyze difficult cases. After a few weeks she got up the courage to ask him for a weekend at her family's villa in Rye, and to her surprise he not only accepted but easily fitted into a household more elegant, presumably, than any he had previously encountered. He brought his law books with him; they must have been the only things that really impressed him.

Ira and Diane were charming to him, of course, but Ione

could see that he bored them, however little they showed it. Unexpectedly she found herself sharply resenting this. Alone with her mother on Sunday night after Tom had returned to town, she suddenly challenged her.

"You were bored stiff with poor Tom, weren't you?"

"Dear me, did I show it?"

"Only to me, of course. Never to anyone else. But it troubles me that you don't see anything in a man like that. He's good and true, and he's going to be a first-rate lawyer. Maybe even a great one. And you don't give a damn. Any more than Dad does." She felt an odd wave of relief as her tone waxed almost strident. "You both only care about how things look. And I care about what they *are*. That's the difference between us!"

"My dear child, what has that young man's goodness and truth and legal aptitude to do with me or your father?" Diane's tone manifested pure reasonableness; she offered no acknowledgment of her daughter's rising temper. "We wish him well, of course, very well. But his virtues are hardly my affair. He doesn't interest me. Except, of course, as a possible husband for my dearly loved daughter. Mothers always see any young man their daughter brings home in that light. We can't help it."

"Well, you can cross Tom off that list. He's not my affair. We work together, that's all. He won't marry until he's a junior partner in some big firm, and then it will be to Miss Mouse. But if I were to take him seriously as a beau, how would you feel about it?"

"We needn't go into that, need we?"

"I'd like to know your criteria."

Diane paused. When she spoke it was after her evident decision that perhaps her daughter *did* need some guidance. "Well, it's my belief that if one has only one life, it better not be spent being bored. The girl who marries your Tom will probably have a kind and faithful husband. But unless she's devoid of imagination she will, after the first thrill of sexual union has passed, have to come to grips with a lifetime of ennui. If she's as hipped on the law as he is, that may be a way out for her."

Ione realized at this with a sudden shock that what her mother was implying was perfectly true: no daughter of hers would ever dream of marrying a man as devoid of humor and imagination as the honest and industrious, the all-deserving Tom. But did that have to mean that she had become a captive of the maternal philosophy, if philosophy it could be called? She found that she was actually trembling with a nervous irritation. She felt an irrational need to shy a stone against the glittering glass fabric of what she wanted desperately to believe was the parental palace of illusion.

"Boredom isn't necessarily the worst thing in the world!" she exclaimed hotly. "Boredom may be only a minor problem in a fundamentally happy marriage to a good and useful man. I don't want my marriage to be like . . ." Here she paused. Was she really going to say it?

"Like your father's and mine?" Diane finished for her coolly. "Go ahead and say it, my dear. It's obviously on your mind. We'd better have it out."

"Well, it does strike me at times," Ione answered in a humbler tone, "that your marriage is based more on the things you don't mention than on the things you do."

"What sort of things?"

"Oh, Mummy, please!"

"What sort of things?" Diane repeated inexorably.

Ione took a deep breath. "Well, Daddy's rather excessive feeling for Adla, for example."

"Ah, at last!" Diane exclaimed as if a great point had been reached. "You catch a whiff of homosexuality?"

"Well, I don't mean they actually *do* anything," Ione murmured miserably.

"They do quite a lot, actually." Diane settled back in her chair. "And I see it's time you and I had a frank talk about these matters. Girls your age chat about everything, I know, so there's no reason for you to suppose that your parents live on a different planet. Your father's generous nature includes both sexes. He has a distinct penchant for handsome young men with which I not only sympathize but which I share. We have both discreetly indulged this penchant. We never asked for it; nature gave it to us. Like alcohol it is harmless unless taken in excess. We have both recognized that we live in a society which is perfectly tolerant of anything that is not blatantly exhibited. We have no wish, in any event, to make a proclamation of things that are essentially private. We regard such follies as 'gay pride' parades or public displays of affection between men and women as the ultimate vulgarity. We enjoy our own warm compatibility and deem our marriage happier than most. It is perfectly true that we care vitally about appearances, perhaps too much, but it's because we both hate ugliness. The world, like your dress and your drawing room, needs to be kept clean and handsome. If you make a good enough replica, it is not only as good as the truth. It can *become* the truth! There we are, my dear. You can take us or leave us. We hope, of course, that you'll take us. But in any event we'll always support you."

When Diane had finished there were several moments of silence during which she gazed with a mildly inquiring look at her daughter while the latter looked down at the floor. When Ione answered her at last her tone was low and apologetic.

"You make me feel that I've been presumptuous and even impertinent, Mummy."

"There's no occasion for that, my dear. Your generation prides itself on its tolerance. I simply expect you to stretch it to cover your parents, which I know is difficult. The most liberal of the young are still capable of being Queen Victoria herself when it comes to judging Mummy and Daddy. I believe that your father and I have been as useful, which is the term you use, as any lawyer, even if that's not saying much. We have tried to contribute a little beauty to a world that signally lacks it, he in how women dress and I in how they live."

This conversation had a considerable effect on Ione's thinking during the rest of her law school career and afterward in her job as an associate in the law firm of Abrams and Sholtz, where she engaged in legal research for the great negligence lawyer Simon Abrams. While she prided herself on being a part of what she liked to think of as the "real world" of injured plaintiffs, ugly lawsuits, and large damages, she was still occasionally glad that it was at least partially balanced by the lacquered world of her parents, whose denizens dressed well and talked well and cultivated charm as a primary virtue. When her mother came to court one day to hear Abrams cross-examine a hostile witness on a subject worked up by her daughter, Ione had to admit that she made the whole procedure seem rather shabby.

She had her own apartment now, a handsome four-room affair beautifully decorated by her mother — her parents always supplemented her moderate salary — and she had developed a lively circle of bright young professional friends who questioned everything from the war in Vietnam to the existence of God, but who were as one in their belief in the importance of "getting ahead."

Her father, whose keen interest in her and deep affection she no longer felt was in any way diminished by his sexual tastes, was much concerned with every aspect of her social life. He was obviously motivated by the desire to see her marry a man whom he would consider worthy of his beloved daughter and one who was apt to make his mark in the world. To Ira, the lawyers in Ione's firm and practice were usually what she called "grubby." But she could never afford not to recognize his impeccable taste or that the young men she met at the family board, those who had clearly been invited for her benefit, were able and honorable youths who bore the aura of success in their different fields and had none of the characteristics of a certain ballet star. Ira Fletcher, like his wife, was always deeper and smarter than one might suspect.

When, therefore, Ione met Michael Sayre at a dinner party at her parents' she knew that he had to be taken seriously, even if his good looks and smooth manners did not assure him of that. He was a young friend of Ira's, a member of an evening discussion group at the Century Club to which both belonged. She couldn't help sending an amused glance down the table at her father, conveying the silent message "Dad, you've hit the jackpot." For Michael was perfect: in looks, in manner, in wit, in sympathy, and in his immediate and enthusiastic reaction to her. He called her at her office the next morning, and they were soon seeing each other on a regular basis. She had had friendships with men, and even one affair, but nothing remotely like this had ever happened to her.

Yet they didn't have an affair, though she made no secret of her willingness. Michael firmly made it clear that with him it was marriage or nothing. He did not in the least imply that he was a virgin, or that he wanted to be one, or that he set the least value on any such state; it was simply, he insisted forcefully, that in his life she had assumed an importance that made any relationship outside of wedlock irrelevant. That was the odd term he used. This, of course, was intensely winning, if it were not mere flattery, and hearing him, she could not doubt his sincerity. It was impossible to doubt his sincerity.

Was this not the man she had been waiting for, the man who would at last unite the seemingly inconsistent worlds of her parents and herself? For like Ira and Diane, he cared for appearances: he showed this in his clothes, in his neatness, in the smooth agility of all his motions, in his careful and beautiful diction, in the ease with which he adjusted himself to any friends to whom she introduced him. On the other hand, his role as a protester against the war in Vietnam had shown him effective and fearless in dealing with mobs and the police, and in his military service in the conflict—for he had refused to reject the draft and he had been decorated for valor. The only inconsistent thing about him was his extraordinary impassivity; he never seemed to lose his temper or even to demonstrate that a right cause or a wrong one had aroused much feeling in him. He was totally consistent in his invariable support of the moral imperative, but bad things, evil things, seemed to him to be simply vermin that had to be efficiently and unemotionally disposed of. Ione imagined him as a heretic hauled before the Spanish Inquisition, coolly pointing out to the court its manifest errors and facing the stake with total equanimity.

She did not like it, however, one evening at a nightclub, when she asked for his opinion of her law firm and received this calm but devastating evaluation:

"I appreciate the argument that every plaintiff is entitled to the best presentation of his case. Lawyers have always cited this as exempting them from any responsibility to society for the havoc that swollen jury awards, vastly exceeding the cost of any damages suffered, have inflicted on our economy. The result is that we perish in paperwork and enormous insurance premiums. An audiologist can't take wax out of your ears without a life history of your illnesses, operations, and allergies."

"And you accuse my firm of causing all that?" she demanded indignantly.

"Simon Abrams is notorious for the way he bamboozles juries. Everyone knows that."

"You're calling him a shyster?"

"I haven't, but I'm quite willing to."

Ione was outraged. "You pretend to care for me, yet you sit there calmly and slander my boss!"

Michael seemed entirely unperturbed. "I don't for a minute admit it's slander, and I fail to see what his being your employer has to do with my assessment of what he may be."

"Because you're calling me a shyster, too!"

"I am not. You look up the law for him. He's certainly entitled to that. It doesn't make you responsible for what he does with it."

"But you think I should quit my job, don't you?"

"I'd be happy if you did, yes. But that's your affair. You must lead your own life, my dear, and not mine. However, I'm always going to be frank with you when you ask me a question. You asked me one tonight."

"Well, I shan't ask you again! You've spoiled my appetite, and I want to go home."

In the taxi she pouted in silence, and at her house she leaped out of the cab without bidding him good night. But there was very little sleep for her in the restless hours that ensued. She finally brought herself to the point of admitting that she would have to choose between her job and Michael. She couldn't go on seeing him and knowing how he viewed her daily occupation. And by morning, pale, exhausted, and defeated, she had made peace with her decision that he was going to be her life. Or at least, she added to herself, with a last fling of defiance, a good part of it.

The very next day she gave notice to her firm that she was quitting her job, offering the acceptable excuse that she was contemplating matrimony, and a few weeks later she applied for and accepted a position with Legal Aid. Michael actually laughed when she informed him of this, and said she hadn't had to go *that* far, but she could see that he was deeply pleased, and in the following month they were married, to the great satisfaction of both their families. The hours at Legal Aid were less arduous than those at her old firm, and she was able to give more time to the babies, a boy and a girl, who made their appearance in the first three years of a blissful marriage. Michael, despite his absorption in his newspaper work, was just as helpful in their domestic duties as she had been sure he would be, and though she never agreed with him that her former boss was a shyster, she knew she had the perfect husband. And when the dazzling offer of the headmastership of Averhill was made to him, he added, if such were possible, another jewel to the crown of his marital perfection.

He told her firmly that he wouldn't consider a position that involved the giving up of her Legal Aid job that the move to Massachusetts would require.

"Oh, my darling," she replied with a gasp, "you can't really compare the headship of a nationally famous school with my representing a few battered wives and petty shoplifters. Of course we're going to Averhill."

"I don't see it that way at all," he retorted stoutly. "I see it as a plush academy for rich kids as opposed to helping the poor and needy in their legal troubles. And not only are you doing a splendid job in Legal Aid—you know you love it."

It was true, Ione reflected ruefully. She *was* doing a decent job, and she *did* love it. A good nurse looked after the children in the daytime, and she was home by six and all the weekend. It was a good life. But she knew what people would say. "He gave up a great career because his selfish wife wanted to keep her trumpery job." She had always believed that in a perfect modern marriage the minor career should bow to the bigger one. She knew that Michael would have surrendered his had she been offered the headship of a great girls' school in another state.

"We needn't argue about it, my dear," she said conclusively. "I shall tell Legal Aid tomorrow that I'm leaving them—whether or not you accept the Averhill offer. So my job will cease to be a factor in your decision."

She went on to insist that their new life at the school would present an exciting challenge for both of them. It was easy for her immediately to see that this attitude was distinctly gratifying to him. Oh, yes, he wanted that job, so long as he could have it with a clear conscience!

"Well, I will say this about it," he commented. "It's really a post for both of us. A headmaster's wife, like a diplomat's, is a partner of her husband."

3

A FULL PARTNER? An equal partnership? Well, for a time Ione had tried to see it that way. The first year at Averhill had been a busy and distracting one for her: rearranging and redecorating the rather worn headmaster's residence, getting the children settled at the local nursery school, meeting the faculty and the faculty wives, acquainting herself with academic ways and traditions. But after that it became apparent that there was a wide and impassable gap between the new headmaster's hectic and crowded days and her own so much more placid ones.

For there was really little enough for a headmaster's wife to do, in the highly organized academic schedule, that seemed worthy of her training in law or even of her general aptitudes. There was the duty of entertainment, to be sure: visiting parents, trustees, and alumni had to be greeted and sometimes fed; "parlor nights," when selected groups of students came to her house for games and cider, had to be organized; faculty wives had to be visited and certain school functions attended. But it was all a bit like being royalty on a very minor scale; a trained and efficient staff did most of the work, and a gracious smile often sufficed as her contribution. Nor did she find any particularly congenial friends among the faculty wives, who struck her on the whole as a rather dreary lot. Everyone was very kind, very helpful, but she was a long way from the glittering world of her parents, which she at last fully appreciated. And the contrast of her life with Michael's zestful and industrious one was not pleasant.

For he had plunged with energy and enthusiasm into what he didn't hesitate to call the challenging job of hauling the school into the modern era. The introduction of coeducation had substantially enlarged the student body; a new dormitory had to be constructed, classrooms expanded, women teachers employed. Courses in science and philosophy had to be added to the schedule, and Michael himself, despite the endless administrative demands on his time, had insisted on teaching a new class in current events that included everything from the arts to government. He even lent an occasional hand in football coaching, and he always attended the Saturday afternoon games with neighboring schools. There was little relief for him, either, on weekends, when he made himself available for conferences with worried parents when he was not traveling to New York or Boston to address alumni on fund drives.

One period each day, however, was rigidly kept for him to be alone with his wife, and that was the half-hour before their bedtime when they discussed the events of the day over a nightcap.

"Darling, you're going to kill yourself if you don't ease up," Ione observed sadly on one such occasion.

"Not so long as I thrive on it!" Michael exclaimed. "So long as I can actually see the barge getting slowly under way as I tug on it, the whole thing is a joy. Arnold of Rugby said there was no happiness on earth comparable to that of a headmaster who feels his school is on the right track."

"And Arnold died of it at age forty-six. Read your Strachey."

"Anyway, I'm sure he died a happy man. But don't worry, my love. I shan't do much dying so long as I have you. Which brings me to something I've been mulling over and which I'm now ready to discuss. I've been very much aware that I cannot expect you to get the same kick out of this Averhill job that I do. And I never forget that you gave up a career you loved for me."

"Oh, Michael, it wasn't all that great," she protested, suddenly mortified at receiving so much credit for so minor a resignation. "I rather liked your thinking I'd sacrificed myself for you. Not that I wouldn't have, anyway."

"Nonetheless, you did it. And I've been racking my brain to find a way of reviving your law career. The big firms in Boston or Springfield are too far to commute to with any comfort, and I'm too selfish and too crazy about you to contemplate your moving there and our being reduced to a weekend marriage."

"Oh, never. Not that."

"But our local burg, Glendon, has a small but reputable

law firm only ten minutes' drive from here. Of course the school's regular counsel is in Boston, but Bates and Harris do our local work, and Joshua Bates is willing to supply you with an office in which to do legal aid work if the idea appeals to you. He won't give you a salary, but you can use his office staff, and he will refer clients to you who can't afford counsel for their wills and mortgages and marital troubles. You won't get paid, and you'll have to get yourself admitted to the Massachusetts bar, but neither of these need trouble you. It'll be the same kind of useful work you did so well in New York."

Ione was touched almost to tears at this evidence of how sensitive he had been to a discontent that she thought she had concealed from him and what pains he had taken in his busy days to work out this plan in her behalf. She could imagine how it must have pained him to use a client's pressure on a dependent local lawyer to benefit his wife, and she had little doubt that he had used his own money to rent that office and buy a share of the staff time. Really, as a husband he was too good to be true!

She motored the next day to Glendon for an interview with Joshua Bates. Glendon was a dreary little town with a few dreary little shop-lined streets, as unlovely as some New England villages could be charming. The nondescript offices of Bates & Harris occupied the second story of a two-story brick shop building. Mr. Bates was polite but reserved; Ione could well feel that he had no interest in legal aid and cared only to oblige the institution that probably supplied him with a good portion of his revenue. The office she would occupy was small and bare; it had probably been used to store files and had just been cleaned out by Mr. Bates's sullen old secretary who showed it to her and no doubt already resented the extra stenographic work that this grand lady from Averhill would demand. Ione could imagine the distrust with which the poor farmers of the neighborhood would regard "Mrs. Fancy Pants" from New York as she looked over their mortgage papers. Driving back into the beautiful Averhill campus, she wondered how she could ever have dreamed of leaving it.

Michael expressed no disappointment when she told him of her decision not to accept the Bates offer, but simply said he would have to find another solution for her. He frowned, however, when she suggested that she might teach a girls' class in English Lit.

"There are no girls' classes, dear. All classes are coed. And keeping order where there may be boys showing off to girls and girls making up to boys requires a practiced hand."

"Oh, I can handle boys."

"The girls may be even harder. The impudent ones—and you can always count on at least one of them to be that—can be very subtle."

"Not subtler than I!"

"Well, let me think it over."

That he did so and took considerable pains about it, she learned later. A plain, severe, and highly competent single lady of fifty, Miss Thompson, headed the English department. She finally—and reluctantly—agreed to let Ione teach one of her classes on Friday mornings, and Ione, much excited, brushed up on the four great tragedies of Shakespeare and the two novels of Henry James that she was assigned to teach. Her students would be sixth-formers, mostly aged seventeen, and presumably mature.

At her first session, the class, of some thirty boys and girls, was silent and attentive—they were taking her measure. A headmaster's wife in the classroom was certainly a novelty. The girls were probably admiring the smart suit that she had worn for the occasion; the boys may have been sniffing out the lawyer behind her very feminine façade. In that initial hour, Ione found herself delivering a monologue on Hamlet's real or feigned madness. But she thought she had been accepted.

The following Friday, with *Othello* as the assigned reading, the class was more responsive. A serious bespectacled lad wanted to discuss just how black Othello was and whether Shakespeare could be accused of racism in depicting him as an unreasonably jealous and insanely violent man. A black girl then retorted angrily that, on the contrary, Othello was seen as a great and noble hero and that Iago was the racist, clearly disapproved of by the playwright. Ione began to fear, as the discussion was noisily joined by others, that any literary criticism was being lost over an issue that had hardly been one in Shakespeare's day. She raised her voice over the clamor.

"We know from Shylock and Marlowe's *Jew of Malta* that anti-Semitism flourished among the Elizabethans, but the number of blacks in England at that time was much too small to have caused any feeling about them one way or the other. The only character who shows any real shock over a white woman's marriage to a black man is Desdemona's father, and the Venetian senate is clearly against him. Iago is not a racist; he simply uses every bit of mud he can get his hands on to sling at Othello. Let us now discuss the question of whether or not Othello is naive in being so easily misled."

A stout, round-faced girl raised her hand. She was Sally Evans, whom Ione knew to be the daughter of a famous backer of Broadway drama. "You're a lawyer, Mrs. Sayre, are you not? Can you tell us why, even if Othello truly believed his wife to be adulterous, he had to strangle her? Couldn't he just have divorced her? Surely adultery was grounds for that in Venice—or even in Cyprus. Wouldn't that have been better than smothering the poor woman with a pillow? And doing it so clumsily that she survived just long enough to try to exculpate him?"

"I may be a lawyer, Sally, but I don't presume to know the Venetian code on domestic relations. But anyway Othello gives us his excuse for such drastic action. He is afraid, if Desdemona lives, that she will betray more men."

"And why is that any business of his?"

"Evidently he felt a moral obligation to protect his own sex. You must remember, Sally, that in Shakespeare's day people were more inclined to impose their morals on others by force than we are. Look at the religious wars of that era."

"But divorce was known to be available! Look at the stink Henry VIII made over Catherine of Aragon."

"But after that he learned a quicker way!" a boy in the back row almost shouted. "He cut off the heads of two wives for adultery! Othello was a piker compared to him!"

Ione felt that the class was getting out of control, and she was relieved when the bell tolled the end of the hour and the class filed out, laughing and loudly talking. But when she tried to make light of the discussion to Miss Thompson, the latter frowned and shook her head.

"They're testing you, Mrs. Sayre, to see just how much they can get away with. I know that Sally Evans. She wasn't in the least interested in what Othello did or didn't do. She was making a joke of the whole thing and a mess of your class. You should have told her roundly that her question was out of order, and if she had persisted in it, to leave the room."

"But, Miss Thompson, wouldn't that have been stifling free discussion?"

"The Evans girl was stifling free discussion. And knew she was doing it, too. Anyway, it's better to overdo than underdo the discipline when you're starting with students you don't know. Once you've made it clear that you won't take any nonsense, then you can ease up a bit. But first things first, Mrs. Sayre."

Nothing would induce Miss Thompson to call her "Ione."

Ione disagreed with the department head's attitude and disliked her, but she found that she had no wish to discuss their exchange with Michael over their nightcap that evening. She was not sure that he would not consider the backing up of his department heads a primary duty of a headmaster.

Two weeks later Ione's classroom was the scene of what she feared Miss Thompson would regard as near anarchy, but which she persisted in viewing as a step forward in unrestricted inquiry. The subject of discussion was the final chapter of Henry James's *The Ambassadors*, when Strether rejects the virtual proposal of marriage offered him by Maria Gostrey on the theory that out of the whole business of his betrayal of trust by urging Chad Newsome to stay on in Paris rather than go home to Woollett he should have got nothing for himself.

"But why shouldn't he marry a fine and attractive woman who will look after him in the city he has come to love?" the bespectacled boy inquired earnestly. "Isn't it a kind of masochism for him to insist on going home to Dullsville and friends who now hate him for having failed them?"

Ione had anticipated the question and had her answer ready.

"You have to see that Maria Gostrey, for all her amiability and good sense, is what James called a *ficelle*. That is a character whose sole function is to elicit from the protagonist information necessary for the reader's understanding of the plot. Gostrey is like the chorus in a Greek drama; she stands aside from the action. Any marriage between a *ficelle*, a piece of string, and a real character is out of the question."

This, of course, evoked a host of protests, and Ione

thought she had reason to believe that things were going well. And they were, until an archly smirking Sally Evans raised her hand.

"I think there may be another reason for Strether's not wanting to marry Maria Gostrey."

"Well, Sally, we'll be glad to hear it."

"Strether has reached a certain age, has he not?"

"You're quite right. Strether is one of the few characters in James whose exact age is given. He's fifty-five."

"And we know what happens to men of that age."

"Do we?" Ione was suddenly uneasy. "What happens?"

"They can't get it up!" Sally, as she almost barked this out, turned to survey the class with a broad smile. An eruption of laughter came, led from the back row where a half-dozen rather ribald boys liked to isolate themselves from the others.

Ione recognized Sally's ploy as a challenge to her authority, but she decided quickly that the way to handle it was to treat it as a serious contribution to the discussion.

"But he had shown himself perfectly willing to marry Mrs. Newsome," she pointed out. "Evidently he saw no problem of impotence there."

"Nor was there!" Sally affirmed triumphantly. "Mrs. Newsome was the kind of grim old New England widow who had probably hated sex anyhow and was glad when her lusty old spouse kicked the bucket. She may even have stipulated that she and Strether would have separate bedrooms."

"You mean she would have insisted on what is called a *mariage blanc*? Possibly."

"And doesn't it dovetail," Sally went relentlessly on, "with Strether's idiotic insistence on seeing Chad's red-hot affair with Madame de Vionnet as a 'virtuous attachment'? All the other characters know they're fucking up a storm!"

Ione, despite the roar of laughter that now emanated from the whole class as well as from the back row, was still determined to handle the crisis in her own way.

"It's interesting in that respect," she pushed firmly on when the laughter had died down, "to note that James has a habit of dropping the curtain on any scene of sexual intimacy. The sole exception may be the one in *The Golden Bowl* where Charlotte and the prince embrace. In James's own life we have no evidence that he ever had a love affair with a person of either sex, though as an aging bachelor he manifested a seemingly homoerotic inclination for handsome young men. That needn't mean, however, that he ever gave into it. You must remember that in his day homosexuality was widely regarded as a mortal sin, and James himself may have felt it as a temptation to be resolutely resisted. He showed little sympathy for Oscar Wilde in the latter's troubles."

This seemed to bring the class to a less ribald mood. One girl asked, "How do you think he felt about Olive and Verena in *The Bostonians*? That was certainly a lesbian relationship, at least on Olive's part."

"But there's no reason to deduce that Olive so much as touched Verena!" Ione exclaimed with conviction. "James was not such a Calvinist as to believe that a feeling was as bad as an action. He greatly, I believe, sympathized with persons who couldn't help their feelings but resisted implementing them. I suspect that his heart went out to Olive, that he saw in her his own inner sadness."

A more orderly discussion of morality and immorality in sexual relations followed, and at the bell Ione felt that she might have even initiated a new step in the communication between teacher and student. But the coolness of Miss Thompson at their next encounter gave her reason to suspect that one of the latter's pets had given her a more lurid version of what had gone on in the class. And once again she forbore from enlightening Michael on this subject at their nightly discussion.

The following Monday morning, when Ione was grading papers in the small office assigned to her in the main classroom building, word reached her that the headmaster wished to see her in his big study below, the primary seat of his administration that she rarely had occasion to visit. In the little anteroom where his dear old chatty and dowdy secretary, Miss Schultze, worked, she was asked if she would mind waiting a minute.

"He's having to break the news to the Anderson boy that his grandmother has just passed away," Michael's fluttery and adoring amanuensis informed her. "Oh, he does that sort of thing so beautifully, Mrs. Sayre! It makes me almost want to lose a loved one to have him tell me."

"Dear me, I trust that won't have to happen."

The study door opened, and a boy drying his eyes came

out. Ione found herself seated before her husband's big desk, with its neatly stacked piles of paper and silver-framed photos of his family. The chamber was hung with pictures of the assembled varsity teams and crews of long past years, and the walls contained shelves of yearbooks and reference volumes. Over the mantel of the empty fireplace loomed the large bad portrait of Michael's clerical predecessor. Ione felt in an odd new and somehow subservient relationship to the gravely attentive man before it. She made an inner resolution to redecorate his office.

"Darling, I'm afraid I have to bring up a rather unpleasant matter," he began. "Miss Thompson has been to see me with a complaint about you. She claims that you have lost control over your class."

Ione bit her lip. "Tell me just what she said, Michael."

He gave her now a roughly accurate account of the classroom discussion that had started over *The Ambassadors*. "Is that a fair version?" he ended.

"More or less. Anyway, it will do. Why did Miss Thompson not come to me with her complaint?"

"She said that she had warned you before, and that you had paid no attention to her. She implied that you were set in your ways and counted on me to back you up."

"And that I may not do?"

"Darling, you put me in a very difficult position."

"I see it. Very well. Tell the old prude I'll give up teaching."

"Ione, dearest, please be reasonable. Nobody's asking

that. Miss Thompson simply wishes me to persuade you to accept her presence in your classroom until such time as order is reestablished."

"And what does she think I have now?"

"I'm afraid she used a strong term. She said you had allowed the class to turn a delicate discussion into a pornographic free-for-all."

"The woman's prejudiced and unreasonable!"

"Ione, please. Is it true that a girl in your class used the f-word?"

"Oh, Michael, the f-word. Why can't you say it?"

"Because I heard it so overused in my naval years that I resolved never to say it except in the very rare cases when it meets the bill. But that's not really the point. The point is that a class where four-letter words are freely flung in the teacher's face is a class either out of control or getting close to it. Miss Thompson may be something of a prude, but she enjoys the reputation of being one of the best English teachers in the New England preparatory schools."

Ione slumped in her chair in a reaction of sudden bitter depression. The great square desk between her and her husband became a barrier; it symbolized in that moment the whole institution that was taking him away from her. And wasn't he right? Wasn't that the worst part of it? The wretched Thompson woman had given her life to teaching; she had even made an art of it. If part of her program was to avoid four-letter words, could a tyro like Ione Sayre really claim that she had a value because she tolerated them? And what had she accomplished but add another burden to the weary shoulders of a heroic and too-loving mate?

"There's enough said, Michael. I'm through with teaching." She rose. "I couldn't teach anyway with that woman in my class. Forgive me for interfering with a schedule that has cost you enough anyway, without adding my peeves."

"Ione, listen to me . . ."

But Miss Schultze had opened the door and was standing there. "I'm sorry, sir, but the bishop has arrived early, ahead of his appointment to see the new window in the chapel. I knew you wouldn't want to keep him waiting."

Ione took a quick step to the door. "It's all right, Amy. I was just leaving, anyway."

Michael moved to stop her. "Ione, please, we've got to talk."

"It's just what we don't have to do. Now go. Please!"

After a brief pause he nodded abruptly and left. Ione turned to Miss Schultze. "Would you please inform Miss Thompson that I am resigning as of today from the teaching staff. She'll have to take back her Friday class. But she'll make no difficulty about that, I assure you."

"Oh, Mrs. Sayre, don't do that!" The secretary's hands were clasped as if in prayer. "You're going to upset your husband terribly. I know it's not my place to tell you, but there's no trouble he won't go to to make you happy at Averhill."

Ione felt a surge of pity for the pleading woman. The poor old thing was probably in love with Michael. And here was his wife actually making a difficult job even more difficult!

"Look, Amy," she said in a kinder tone, "you must know that things will go more smoothly here if the headmaster's wife doesn't interfere with the teaching policies of the school."

When Miss Schultze nodded slowly after a momentary pause, Ione had the mortification of suspecting that her problems had been the subject of serious discussions between her husband and his confidential secretary.

Later that day she herself had a serious discussion with Michael. She took a high and firm tone with him. She took the blame for having thrust herself into the academic program, but criticized him for not having checked her. She reduced his protests to a resigned silence and affirmed that it was her duty now to find a more fitting role for herself in the Averhill community. She ended with a ringing assertion of her conjugal devotion, and that night they made passionate love.

She now resolved to accept her position as a faculty wife, and, as a start, to cultivate the society of the other faculty wives. She organized a book class to meet for a buffet lunch at her house on alternate Mondays that was soon well attended. She decided to also include the women teachers, though all but one declined, on the alleged ground of a too busy schedule, but for the real reason—at least Ione suspected—that they considered the faculty wives a bunch of old tabbies. She also invited the husbands of any women teachers, but only one of these, a shrill gossipy type, accepted.

The first book selected for discussion was *The Scarlet*

Letter, and it was followed by *Madame Bovary* and then *The House of Mirth*. Ione was a bit nonplussed to discover that the ladies tended to confine their "criticism" of classic fiction almost exclusively to the expression of their like or dislike of the characters involved. It was as if Hester Prynne or Emma Bovary or Lily Bart were up for membership in the book class. And all would have been turned down, even over the acid dissent of the solitary faculty husband.

In an effort to stir up some more lively comment she proposed *The Ambassadors* for the next meeting. She had seen what students could make of it; it might be interesting to see what an older group would.

Mrs. Warren, the senior member of the class, wife of the sexagenarian head of the Latin department, who, with the aid of a fortune inherited from her wealthy New York clan, had built a grotesque gothic mansion near the campus, was a berouged, bewigged, would-be grande dame who deemed herself the leading intellectual of the group on the basis of a slim volume of privately printed verse. She took it upon herself to lead the discussion.

"Of course, in my youth, it was taken for granted that any young man who paid more than a tourist's visit to Paris was there for an immoral reason. He was naturally expected to come home and go into a proper business and marry a proper girl. That was the system, and who is to say that it didn't work? Look around you, and see what we have today. Strether was a perfect ass to assume that Chad Newsome had the slightest moral obligation towards a designing and married French

woman ten years his senior. There was a time in history when
such women were whipped at the cart's tail. And good enough
for them, too. I'd have saved a few lashes for Strether himself. He actually believed that a young man should give up his
home, his family, and his business, and tie himself to the apron
strings of an old tart because she has taught him how to enter
a theatre box gracefully after the show had started!"

"Oh, but Mrs. Warren, you're leaving out love!" protested Mrs. Littleton, the pretty new bride of a handsome
physics teacher. "It is love that has turned the crude young
Chad into a charming and poised gentleman. Strether has
seen that Chad has attained the sublime in life and can't bear
to have him give it up."

The room now joined in heartily. But the tide was clearly
in Mrs. Warren's favor, and the romantic views of the physics
teacher's wife were in the minority. Ione suspected that there
was some feeling in the group that the latter was too junior
a member to be quite so vociferous, but there was no doubt
that they were sincere in their belief that the novel perni-
ciously promoted adultery and expatriatism. She decided at
last to protest.

"I can't help thinking that some of you may be missing
what is really going on in Strether's mind and heart. He
sees that Chad is basically a child of Woollett and that he is
bound in time to break with Madame de Vionnet and take
himself home to Mummy and the family business. He knows
he can't prevent this; he simply wants to express as forcefully as he can to Chad how much the young man owes to

the wonderful woman who has taught him all the beautiful things that his drab hometown hasn't. Strether knows how his own vision of Paris has made a garden of the desert of his life, and he hopes that Chad will at least take some of that vision home with him."

Everyone in the room listened respectfully—after all, she *was* their hostess—but she could tell that her interpretation failed to impress. Strether had told Chad that he would be a villain if he deserted his Parisian mistress, had he not? How could any of them get around that? Wasn't Averhill *their* Woollett? How could they ever admit a vision of Paris that threatened their satisfaction with what they were?

That night was "parlor night," when some forty students (different dormitories were invited on different nights) invaded the big hall and two living rooms of the headmaster's house to play games or join sing-alongs or even to dance to taped music. Ione and a couple of faculty wives acted as hostesses, but that evening she pleaded a slight headache and sat in an isolated corner with a pale, skinny, and awkward fourteen-year-old lad who worked on a large and difficult jigsaw puzzle spread out on a card table. He had worked on it on a previous parlor night, and Ione had seen to it that the card table, with folded legs, had been placed on a shelf in a closet so that the unfinished puzzle was preserved. The boy, Berty Dean, was an obvious loner who had presumably found it difficult to adjust himself to boarding-school life.

"Do you mind my helping you with it?" she asked him, smiling. "Together we might be able to finish it tonight."

"Oh, I don't mind at all, Mrs. Sayre. It was very kind of you to preserve it for me."

"You like jigsaw puzzles?"

"I like this one."

"Why this one, particularly?"

The boy's large dark eyes seemed to betray a struggle with caution. Was this lovely lady really on his side? Could she be trusted? "Because it takes me away from here. When I fit a piece into the picture I'm doing something that has nothing to do with school."

"It takes you home perhaps. Are you homesick, Berty? It's very natural. I sometimes am myself."

"But this is your home, isn't it?"

"I sometimes wonder."

He gave her a tiny smile. Evidently, she *could* be trusted. "Not liking where you are doesn't have to mean you're homesick."

"I suppose it could even mean you're schoolsick."

But she shouldn't be getting into this, and they both turned their attention to the puzzle. A sing-along had started in the hall, and the noise distracted her.

> The sons of the prophet
> were hardy and bold,
> And quite unaccustomed to fear,
> But the bravest of all,
> at least so I am told,
> Was . . .

"I really do have a headache now," she murmured, half to herself, and rising and apologizing to one of the presiding faculty wives, she went upstairs to her room to lie down.

The image of the unhappy and ungainly boy struggling to escape the jeers and pokes of his nasty contemporaries by fitting together pieces of pasteboard to create a landscape that had no merit other than its not being Averhill haunted her with its suggestion of a parallel to her own case. But of course he had no Michael to love him, and when the latter came suddenly into the room she sat up and threw her arms about him.

"My poor darling," he exclaimed. "I heard you had to leave those awful games. Are you all right?"

"Oh, I'm fine," she assured him. "Just a bit tired, that's all. Get me a drink, will you. I want to talk to you."

When he came back with their drinks, she was already out of bed, seated in a chair and ready for a serious discussion.

"Ever since my fiasco as a teacher," she began, "I've been doing a good bit of thinking, not only of my role in our lives, but of yours."

"So have I," he concurred. "My role seems to have been pretty well determined, but it's been very much on my mind that it's been determined at the expense of yours."

"I shouldn't so much mind that if I could be sure that you were on the right path for yourself."

"You're not content with what I'm doing here? I can hardly blame you. I am constantly running into problems that make me see how inadequately I was prepared to be a headmaster."

"No, no, I don't mean that at all!" she emphasized. "You're doing great as a headmaster. Everyone agrees to that. Everyone, that is, but that ass, Spencer, and with him it's just jealousy and spite. No, what I'm getting at is that I have the highest ambition for you. I'm very proud of your record here, but I don't see Averhill as your final goal. I want much more for you. Much more, my darling."

"Dear me. How far will you take me? To the White House?"

"Don't laugh at me. But it's true that I set no limits. You might be the head of a great university."

He shrugged. "Well, let's leave all that to the future. In the meantime I have my hands full at Averhill."

"Well, of course you have. But haven't you already, and in only three years, basically achieved what you set out to do?"

"How do you mean?"

"Girls are admitted now. That was the great step. And Latin made optional after the third form. And Catholic and Jewish students exempted from compulsory chapel. Racial prejudice is down, and kids no longer get suspended for the dirty talk they've learned at their own fireside. Weekends home are allowed once a term, and you even have a fairy as chaplain—"

"Darling, your tone!" Michael interrupted reproachfully.

"Oh, I know, I know, but when I've had to mind my p's and q's all day and night in your temple of political correctness, it's a relief every once and a while to play the philistine."

"But that term! And from you!"

"All right, call him gay, homosexual, whatever you want. I know he's still in the closet, but something tells me he's about to pop out. Anyway, my point is that the main bastions of the old days have been leveled. Isn't it at least time to consider your next step?"

"Darling, if I stop for a minute, I may fatally lose momentum. I might indeed lose all. What I've accomplished so far is as precarious as a clearing in the jungle. If the bulldozers are idle for even a month, regrowth will swallow it up. I don't know when the time will come for me to consider a change, but it's a long way away. And now, if you'll forgive me, I'll go back to my study to prepare for tomorrow's class. You should finish your drink and get some sleep to cure that headache."

Ione was silenced for the time being, but she was glad she had broken the ice on a subject that she had no intention of dropping. She was determined to cling to the notion that his real job at the school had been largely accomplished. It allowed her to indulge in a dream that the time was approaching when a headmaster could be tempted, like Alexander the Great, to look about for new lands to conquer. She tried to see this in the light of a natural desire to spur her husband on to the achievement of higher and nobler goals and not to a selfish yearning on her part to escape the ennui of her life at Averhill. She detested the idea that she might be motivated by any concern for her own welfare. At the same time, however, she was too honest and too intelligent not to see both sides of her dilemma.

She was much relieved, therefore, when something in the next week happened to glorify Michael's alternative to remaining a headmaster in such a way as to reduce to nothing any question of a benefit to herself. She had gone to New York to attend a big dinner party celebrating her parents' wedding anniversary, and she found herself seated next to Timothy Armstrong, chairman of the board of the famed Gladwin Foundation. Michael had had to remain in Averhill for class reunion day.

Well trained by her mother in how to handle tycoons, Ione induced the stout, ivory-haired, gravelly-voiced distributor of millions to talk about himself. He at once proceeded to complain about the troubles of his day. The director of his foundation had just received a diagnosis of lung cancer and would have to retire.

"It's hard on him, of course," he conceded, "but it's also hard on me."

"Because you now have to find a successor for him?" she asked. "But that shouldn't be too difficult. Anyone you ask will jump at the chance. It's a great position."

"Yes, but here's the problem, Mrs. Sayre. If you're looking for the head of a university or a hospital or a museum, you retain a headhunter who will provide you with a list of eligible professors, doctors, or curators. But a foundation head doesn't have to belong to any special category. The whole world, so to speak, can apply, and you're faced with a list as long as the telephone directory."

"You couldn't limit it to officers in other foundations?"

"And rule out some great scientist or statesman or industrialist? Would that be doing our duty to the public? Giving away money requires wisdom and caution and worldly common sense, which are qualities to be found in all fields of leadership."

"Even in private boarding schools?" she ventured to ask with a smile, as if in jest.

"Like Averhill? Why not? By the way, I hear great things about your husband. They say that school is leading all the others in New England now in student applications."

"I'm glad people speak well of him. He's really working his tail off. I worry about his killing himself." Here she appeared to be continuing her little joke. "I wish your foundation would rescue him. Mightn't he do for you?"

"Oh, he'd qualify all right." The look he now gave her was a chairman's look. "But he wouldn't think of leaving Averhill, would he? He's pretty well stuck up there, isn't he?"

"Oh, he might be detached," she replied in a tone more matter of fact. "He was hired to bring the school up to date, and he's pretty well done that. A new challenge might be just the thing he needs."

"I'll make a note of that. I really will."

He had to talk now to the aggressive old lady on his other side whose imperious poke reminded him that the table was turning.

She decided to make no mention of this exchange when she returned to school. She knew that a good deal of work would have to be done on Michael before he could be induced to leave Averhill, and she would need a plan and the time to form one. But she had followed tensely the discussion between Michael and Donald Spencer about the proposed sports plaza and had seen in it the seed of a major conflict between the headmaster and the board of trustees. If Michael should try to temper the project, which seemed only too likely, and Spencer should dig in his heels, which seemed equally probable, and the board should support Spencer, which they were only too apt to do where large sums were promised, might not Michael, strongly backed by a loving spouse, pull out altogether? And move on to a glorious career in a city where he and Ione could both do the work they loved? Who said that one couldn't have one's cake *and* eat it?

Donald Spencer, when he next came up to the school, was unpleasantly surprised to discover that the headmaster had, in only a few days' time, made a thorough study of his architect's rough draft for the proposed sports plaza and already sketched out with his own hand some drastic alterations. The gymnasium was reduced in size by a good half and located off-campus on the edge of a declivity in such a way that the top two stories visible from the main school oblong were on a level with the other buildings, while its bulk, with the great hall and swimming tank, discreetly descended the slope in back without dwarfing other structures. The indoor hockey rink was abandoned but the pond near the school that was now used for the sport when iced over was provided with heated changing rooms. The nine-hole golf course was abandoned, as were the oval seats around the football field, but new wooden stands for onlookers were specified. The tennis and squash courts were not changed.

"Well, if ever a gift horse was stared in the mouth, this is it," Donald expostulated.

"That equine is being saved a great deal of money," Michael assured him.

"And since when did I ask you to be my treasurer?"

"You didn't, of course. But you can hardly expect a headmaster to hold his tongue when he sees the basic character of his institution being altered."

"I expect a headmaster not to hurl a donor's money back in his face! My project will put this school right up at the top of the New England prep schools where it belongs!"

"We have been into that already, Don. You and I will never see eye to eye, I fear. We must leave the decision to the board."

"And how do you propose to persuade them that my plan changes the character of the school?"

"If they don't see it themselves, I'm afraid I can't. Your plan, by placing the major emphasis of Averhill on sports, or at least giving it that appearance, is fundamentally anti-intellectual. Appearances are only too apt to become realities."

"And all this you deduce from the simple improvement of the athletic facilities available to students?"

"It goes deeper than that, Donald." Michael's dry, cool, impassive tone angered the chairman, suggesting as it did that if his interlocutor would only divest himself of vulgar prejudices for a minute he would have to agree. "A worship of sports can be a challenge to the basic aims of academe. Instead of individual thinking, instead of a fearless questioning of even the most accepted principles, the cult of the muscle and competitive games looks to robotlike teamwork and subservience to a leader."

"You would abolish athletics altogether?" Donald glimpsed an argument that could destroy the headmaster.

"Certainly not. I used the word "cult" advisedly. The emphasis on athletics, like most academic affairs, is a matter of degree. I do not think it's irrelevant to keep in mind that dictatorships have always favored sports as a convenient way of drilling young men into tightly organized and obedient units. I may be oversensitive but I sometimes catch a faint whiff of *Heil Hitler* in the roar of a crowd in a stadium."

"Are you calling me a fascist, Sayre?"

"I'm simply pointing out that there's a bit of that in all of us. We have to watch it. I myself find even the power of a schoolmaster a dangerous instrument."

"You'll find it that if you try to use it against my board of trustees."

"Some of whom already deplore your frank espousal of the late Senator McCarthy's views."

"Oh, you discuss that with them, do you? No doubt some of the younger ones have been brainwashed by indurated liberals who refuse to credit the infiltration of our government by reds. But if you think you're going to get anywhere with that crap with the sounder members of our board, you're riding for a fall."

Michael was at least aroused to an argument ad hominem. "Which of us fought in Vietnam, Donald?"

"With that I'll leave you!" the other exclaimed wrathfully. "It's useless for me to discuss the matter further with you. We can leave it to the board."

And he strode out of the room.

"What it really gets down to," Michael explained to Ione that night, "is who's going to run Averhill, him or me."

"What a curious man he is," she mused. "Why, with his millions, does he care so?"

"Ah, that's his whole life."

It was. Or an essential part of it. Donald's first hard battle in life had been at Averhill, and he liked to think he had won it, though only after a considerable struggle. The struggle had come as a rough shock to him, for up to his boarding school entry age of thirteen he had ruled the roost as eldest son in the big square brownstone mansion on Sixtieth Street with its fringe of Egyptian hieroglyphics on the façade and which, unusually for Manhattan, had been occupied by more than one generation of Spencers. Donald's parents had shared it with his widower paternal grandfather, and when the old gentleman had died his mother, the lovely Adelaide, had stripped off the hieroglyphics and redecorated the interior in elegant French eighteenth-century style, satisfying her long frustrated fine taste. His father, Howard, though totally subservient and under the spell while he lived off his own father, the famous banker Lloyd Spencer, whose bedroom the motherless boy had shared up to his own marriage, had nonetheless, on Lloyd's death, transferred much of this loyalty and devotion to his stronger-minded mate. He had insisted on retaining, however, the management of their oldest boy, whose development and education he tightly controlled, leaving her virtual sole charge of the two younger boys, who though hearty and handsome, shared little of the brains or aggressive manners of their plainer, stouter elder brother whom they were bullied into obeying.

Howard Spencer, a charming, kindly man who seemed to apologize to the world for being so wealthy, suffered from the peculiar obsession that his destined role in life was to be the needed link between his tycoon father and his future tycoon oldest son. For this, by efforts almost heroic, he had turned himself away from the publishing career of which he had dreamed and become instead the competent if not brilliant chairman of the great bank his father had founded with the duty to pass it on intact to his son. But if he had supplemented whatever he lacked as a banker with his fine selection of able officers, he had shown less judgment in his indulgence of every quirk of his chosen heir. It can be argued in his favor that he spotted early the remarkable talents of the boy whom he took with him on all his business trips to check on companies his bank underwrote: the boy's aptitude for accounting, his quick grasp of administrative problems, his imaginative concept of the industrial field. But less can be said for his theory that a natural genius should be left undisturbed to develop as it would.

Donald was the constant companion of a father who bought him everything he wanted and applauded his every idea. Not only was he taken on the business trips, but on cruises on the family yacht he shared the huge paternal cabin (his mother suffered from sea sickness and remained happily ashore) and relayed to the captain his father's orders, which he sometimes changed to suit himself. Even after the younger brothers had developed the muscle to oppose him physically, the habit of obedience and their father's unfailing support of him quelled any but silent retaliation. And at day school in the city Donald was spared any violence that his arrogance aroused in his classmates by the fact that they were at all times in a closely supervised classroom or playground.

Adelaide was always aware that her eldest son needed disciplining, but she found her usually compliant husband as steel in this area, and she finally renounced interference and concentrated her love and care on the younger boys, whom she adored and whose poor performance in school she sought to improve by her own tutoring at home. The contrast of Donald's high grades was painful to her, and there began to develop between mother and son a kind of mute hostility of which only the two of them were aware. Donald knew that the household contained one critic whom he could never impress, and he resented it, and Adelaide, ashamed of a dislike that seemed unnatural to the mother in her, tried to convince herself that she would love the boy as soon as he was straightened out by a boarding school and that her recommendation of his being sent to one was for his good and not her own.

Indeed it took some persuasion, for Howard balked at the idea of separating himself from his favored child. What brought him around in the end was the argument offered by friends in the Downtown Association, where he regularly lunched, that a boy who hadn't been to an acceptable prep school would be socially handicapped at an Ivy League college.

Thrown to the lions in the arena of Averhill, as Donald would later describe it, he found himself subject to the jeers and fisticuffs of boys who were not in the least impressed by his family's wealth. The ones who themselves came from rich backgrounds saw it as no reason for boasting, and the ones who didn't saw it as something to be resented. All agreed that it was no excuse for clumsiness at sports or oddity of appearance, and Donald was hazed more than the other new kids, and as he had not learned the art of making friends he was isolated indeed. Worst of all was the bitter humiliation of the nickname "Peewee," attributed by the boys' discovery in the shower room that his private parts had been slower than normal in their development. At this his will was almost broken, and he was on the verge of appealing to his father to bring him home.

What intervened to prevent this was the sudden and totally unexpected support that he derived from Michael Sayre, the handsomest and most popular member of his form. Hearing another boy spitting the hated epithet at poor Donald, he grabbed him roughly and shook him hard. "That's a filthy thing to call him for something that's not his fault!" he exclaimed, and for a few days afterward he showed his endorsement of Donald, walking beside him on the way to chapel, sitting next to him in the dining hall, and giving him pointers in football practice. The horrid epithet was heard no more. Michael had made it unfashionable, and boys follow fashion as docilely as men.

Donald for the first time in his life was overwhelmed with affection for someone other than himself. Michael now represented to him everything that he would like to be and wasn't. He tried to fancy himself as a kind of partner in a glorious friendship: together they would dominate the form and ultimately the whole school. But Michael, like a doctor whose patient is cured, moved quietly out of Donald's life. He had his own circle of friends, the inner crowd of the form, and though they treated Donald civilly, he would never be really one of them. It was hard but it had to be faced. He would have to make do with what he could find outside the sacred circumference.

At any rate Donald would remain at Averhill. There was no further question of appealing to his father. Averhill was clearly a test of manhood, and this was a test that Donald was determined to pass. He scanned the school, the students, the faculty, the curriculum to determine just where and how the institution could be "had." Sports were the most obvious path to popularity and esteem, but in them he was barely adequate. If one could excel in just one, it would help, and he concentrated on fencing, where there was very little competition and in which he could enjoy the fantasy of actually killing his opponent. There was a school weekly to which he could become a regular contributor, reporting on games and other events, and a debating society in which he was sure he could ultimately star. Finally there was the dramatic society in which, without the looks for a hero, he could train himself to play villains and even buffoons. Oh, yes, there were opportunities for one who cared.

Over the years before his graduation, Donald achieved a considerable status in the student body. He adopted the role of a mordant critic whose bite was always qualified by wit and just a hint of concealed benevolence. As the boys grew older and began to take account of the outside world, he made himself something of an expert in politics, reading newspapers and periodicals, and found that he was at his best with the students of rich parents and with his always watching father by taking a conservative view and posing as the weary and well-documented realist who saw through the hypocrisy of the idealist and the reformer while flattering his listener with the assumption that he was too smart not to agree. It became almost a mark of superior sophistication to be included in Donald Spencer's set. At the end of his fifth-form year he nursed hopes of being elected by the fifth and sixth forms (the latter was the graduating class) as one of the seven prefects who assisted the faculty in the administration of the school in their final year.

He had no chance, he recognized, of being chosen as the senior prefect. That was apt to go to the captain of one of the athletic teams and one not so weak academically as to incur the veto which the headmaster held over the election outcome. Of the three or four likely candidates Michael Sayre seemed the most favored, but it was by no means a sure thing, any more than was Donald's chance of being chosen one of the lesser prefects. Canvassing was frowned upon but it surreptitiously existed, and Donald decided to make full use of it even with a student of such reputed rectitude as his former champion, Michael. Had not Michael helped him once, and when it had been unpopular to do so?

He fell in with Michael one afternoon when he spied the latter walking down the path to the river for crew practice.

"I thought you were a shoo-in for senior, Mike, but some guys tell me that Ted Ives is running you close," he began.

"Are people discussing that?" Michael demanded curtly. "They shouldn't and they know they shouldn't."

"Well, do you want to have a dope like Ives our boss? Do we have to lie down and let his snotty clique run over us?"

"If Ives is chosen, that's okay with me." Saying which Michael broke into a jog as if to terminate an unwelcome discussion. But Donald kept up with him.

"Ives is seeking votes right and left. Of course he shouldn't. But isn't he forcing us to do the same thing?"

"Two wrongs don't make a right."

"Mike, for Pete's sake listen to me! I can swing six votes for you which should put you over the top. And if you in turn will back me up, you'll have a damn good and loyal executive officer!"

Michael stopped at this and faced him.

"Look, Spencer. I take for granted that any prefect elected will be a loyal aide to any senior elected. And I'm not going to discuss with anyone whom I'm going to vote for. All I'll tell you is that I don't give a rat's ass if you're elected or not. And now, if you'll forgive me, I want to jog on to the river."

This was delivered in a flat dry tone that expressed even more forcefully the contempt in which the speaker held the person addressed. When Michael resumed his jog, Donald did not follow him.

Michael *was* elected senior prefect, and Donald as one of the lesser ones, but Donald in their final year did not show himself the supporter of his superior that he had offered. His enthusiasm for the champion of his early years was now replaced by envy and resentment that intensified by having to be hid if he did not wish to appear irrationally hostile to a universally popular figure. He had to content himself with minor sniping to other prefects over any slip in the conduct of the admired senior, which was so little noticed that the object of the sniping was the only one to know he had a real enemy. And when, seventeen years later, the board of Averhill, of which Donald was then a member though not yet chairman, was presented by its search committee with the name of Michael Sayre as the successor chosen to the retiring headmaster, Donald had bitterly to recognize that any opposition to so popular a candidate, lacking specific grounds for complaint, might seriously diminish his influence on trustees hitherto awed by his large grants. The vote for Michael was unanimous, and when, shortly after his appointment, Donald himself was raised to the chairmanship, he established a working relationship with the new headmaster that both men knew was a practical necessity and that both men knew was simply a form.

Donald, with the total backing of a father powerful even in his retirement and with a great bank virtually at his disposal, had used his own financial ability to enormous advantage, and while still in his thirties had, like a number of his contemporaries, accumulated a fortune of many millions. He had been less happy in his marriage, though not from the cause of his hated nickname at school, which maturity had taken care of. At twenty-nine he had decided, with very little previous experience with women in his busy life, that Caroline Kip, quiet, reserved, pretty, conventional, the devoted and submissive daughter of a drearily respectable couple of Knickerbocker descent, was just the wife he needed to give him children to inherit his fortune without interfering in the hectic schedule of his many deals and trips. He was enough of a realist to recognize that he was looking for docility, and not afraid to call it just that, but not perspective enough to know that it was a quality that women of an earlier time merely feigned. He did not see, either, that Caroline, anxious to escape a dull home and not presented with many eligible admirers, understood just what he was after and was only too ready to supply the appearance of it. But our motivations are rarely simple: she wanted the money, yes, but she also wanted love, and she had almost succeeded in persuading herself that Donald was the prince of her dreams—perhaps in disguise—and he did at times look something like a frog. At any rate, they married.

Trouble was not long in coming. Donald was accustomed on Saturday afternoons to playing squash at the Racket Club, after which he would have drinks with his friends at the bar, and if there happened to be a group dining there, join them. Caroline went along happily with his business trips—she never objected to anything connected with his work—but if he was home she certainly did not expect to spend her Saturday nights alone. She objected in vain; she made scenes in vain. He would retire to his study and lock the door. He was like a heavy barge that would cease its barely perceptible moving the moment one stopped pushing: it was impossible to get any way on.

She hoped things might improve with the birth of their twins, a boy and a girl, but Donald, who was one who took no interest in children before they reached their teens and not much then, was always too busy to push their perambulator in the park, even on a weekend. She appealed at last to her mother-in-law, who was more than willing to give her oldest son a piece of her mind.

"You have a lot to learn about women, my dear," she told him. "Caroline is not as hard to please as you like to make out. She's not asking for much, simply that you give her more of your company. If you give her that, you'll soon find out, as many husbands have, that she doesn't need that much, and you'll have your sacred freedom back. Maybe even too much of it."

"It seems to me that I've already given her all a reasonable woman could want," Donald retorted, angered as always by the maternal jabs. "How many wives have a car and chauffeur at their disposal, a penthouse in town, a villa in the country, servants galore and a princely allowance?"

"Silly boy, silly boy. Don't you realize that she wants you to give her something that it *hurts* you to give? She wants a concession on your part. Something that shows you love her."

"Well, I'm afraid she's going to have to learn to take me as I am."

"Oh, she'll never learn that."

"Didn't she agree to take me for better or for worse?"

"Women knocked out the 'worse' when they got the vote. You're out of date, dear."

"Then it's a pity they ever got it!"

"Don't be a fool, Donald. You'll wreck everything. You know how to run a business. Learn to run a home."

But he wasn't going to heed her. His mother had never really subscribed to the Spencer values, at least as he defined them. Oh, she liked the money well enough, that was evident in the spending his father never checked. Asked by a friend once if she had ever felt guilty about having so much when others had so little, Adelaide's much-quoted reply had been: "Yes, I did at first, but as there was nothing I could do about it, I decided to make myself thoroughly comfortable." And she certainly had! There was something in her air, in her attitude, that implied that if men ruled the downtown world, they had done well to leave the truly important things, the arts and the art of living, to women. She had no loyalty to the lares and penates of moneymakers. When Donald had once protested after she had invited and paid a famous radical novelist—some said a card-carrying communist—to address her book class, she had simply told him to "grow up."

Caroline, advised by her mother-in-law, began to accept her husband, but it was a silent, moody acceptance. She spent most of her time with the twins now, and hardly seemed to notice whether Donald stayed home or went out. Sometimes, when they had a social engagement, she at the last moment would refuse to go with him on the obviously false excuse of a migraine, and nothing could convince her to change her mind. Still, their married life had the outward appearance of normality, and Donald supposed that this would have to be enough. And it might have been without the episode of the Connecticut house.

Donald's mother had a curious apprehension that the family fortune was not destined to last, at least not in its present bulk, and she used serenely to make occasional purchases of things that would enable them to be comfortable in a reduced scale of living. One of these was a charming little eighteenth-century house in Connecticut, a colonial gem on the edge of a village green. There she would sometimes go for summer weekends, taking Caroline and the twins. Donald's father, who cheerfully paid for everything his wife desired, remarked to his oldest son with a chuckle, "Fortunately, I am still rich enough to afford your mother's economies."

Caroline loved the house, and when her mother-in-law tired of playing Marie Antoinette at her *hameau*, as Donald sourly put it, she asked her husband, who always took title in his own name, to deed it to her daughter-in-law. Howard, of course, instantly complied, but in the Spencer tradition he gave the place to Donald rather than to his wife. To him it was the same thing.

The house was not heated and was closed all winter, so that, the transfer having taken place in October, there was no idea of Caroline spending a weekend there before late spring. And it so happened that only weeks after Donald took title he received a magnificent offer for the property, which had become necessary to a developer who was taking over the entire little village for a huge retirement home. In accordance with every precept of his economic philosophy, Donald promptly sold it, delaying just long enough to sweeten the already succulent offer.

He saw no reason to tell Caroline. He concluded that over the ensuing months she might even lose her interest in the house. But he was a bit nervous about it. She had spoken of it with real feeling, and he had even wondered if she might wish to heat it and live in it permanently, expecting him only for weekends and putting their marriage on that basis.

He did not know it when, on an early spring day, she drove up to Connecticut to show a friend the house. She was faced with a vacant lot. The developer's bulldozer had preceded her.

The scene to which she subjected her husband on her return ended all possibility of a happy union in the future. She screamed at him that he had taken the one thing she loved of the family properties and destroyed it for no other reason than to hurt and humiliate her. He had coldly insisted that he had treated the house like any other asset in his portfolio, disposing of it for a price that would almost surely never come again. He offered to hold the cash proceeds for any purchase that she might ask. She said that she wanted nothing and would take the twins and return to her own family.

In the end she didn't do this. Her parents didn't want her, and she had no grounds for a divorce. Adelaide Spencer intervened, and Caroline was persuaded that the best thing for her and her children was to remain under the protection of the Spencers and their wealth. In a lawsuit Donald would have fought her with all his clout and money; in a reconciliation he would leave her strictly alone and support her in style. What else could she do?

Well, she could drink, and that, alas, she did. She isolated herself more and more from her friends and became a shadowy figure rarely seen and talked about with shaken heads. She suffered from recurrent severe depressions and spent much of her time in a psychiatrist's office. Adelaide saw a great deal of her and kept her from going seriously off the tracks. The two children, who had inherited a good slice of their father's toughness, did surprisingly well with all the governesses and tutors and servants that money could supply. Even Donald, guided more and more by a mother whom his domestic crisis had hoisted into a position of necessary supervision, took a more proper paternal interest in them, and their mother faded into a frail ailing presence that could be kissed in the morning and forgotten during the day.

Donald was too clear an observer not to feel the contrast of the failure of his home life with the success of his business one, nor could he escape the bleak recognition that the only common denominator between the two was the hostility he had incurred in both. He was sensitive enough to be hurt by this, and he found himself looking around for some way or ways to establish a more favorable reputation for his name and career. Why should a man like Michael Sayre get all the glory in a world largely managed by men like Donald? Donald wanted a good name; he wanted people to point to his good works. Had not his creed been that money could buy anything? Why should it not buy him that? Philanthropy had always a good name, and what bought it but money?

The obvious object of his bounty was Averhill. Any gift to his alma mater, Harvard, would be lost in the sea of that institution's vast wealth. Moreover he had a definitive nostalgia for his years at preparatory school. The one thing in his life that he could romanticize was his own gallant fight to rise from a state of ridicule and persecution to a prefectship, all accomplished by his own willpower and without the aid of a penny of the family fortune. The school had several rich trustees but none who were able or willing to do as much as he. As a big enough donor he might identify his own name with that of the academy.

The election of Michael to the headmastership had been an ugly shock to Donald, as he saw his own prospect of fame dimmed in relation to the shining reputation of this new star in the field of education. The only practical way of handling the situation was to ally himself to the new head in such manner as to create the illusion that they constituted an equal partnership. Everyone knew that they had been fellow formmates—could the myth not be spread that the board chairman and the headmaster had been joined in a lifelong union dedicated to the growth and glory of Averhill?

It had not, however, worked out that way. Donald had not foreseen the sweeping changes that Michael would inaugurate, the credit for which could not be attributed to anyone but the headmaster. Donald himself had been strongly opposed to almost all of them. He hated the admission of girls to the student body, the loss of preference for the sons of graduates, the increase of racial and religious diversity, the general relaxation of discipline, the presence of what he considered radicals on the faculty. He firmly believed in an Averhill as much as possible like the one he had attended. He had suffered a loss of prestige in the defeats he had met opposing these measures from a board that seemed as hypnotized by the headmaster as the children of Hamelin by the Pied Piper. It had been to regain his authority over the trustees that he had devised his great sports plan. And now the insufferable Michael was proposing to cut it into slivers and was actually making some headway with the younger and more liberal members of the board!

It was too much, really too much.

But wait! Arriving early at his Wall Street office one morning he found the school's lawyer waiting to see him. He brought news of a lawsuit threatened against the school by the parents of a boy who claimed he had been the victim of a homosexual rape. As Donald skimmed through the counsel's memoranda outlining the nature of the case, he felt a warming of his heart. Sexuality was the gift of an inscrutable god, accorded to man for his damnation as well as his reproduction. Many a great man had stubbed a fatal toe on it. Why should Michael Sayre not be another?

4

MICHAEL WAS EVER AFTER to refer to the boy Elihu Castor as Eris, because it was she who cast the apple of discord into the banquet of the gods.

Elihu, as a fourth-former and fifteen, was a black-haired, chubby lad of a lounging physical attitude, with large, deeply apprehensive red-brown eyes, the pampered only child of a rich, stout, opinionated mother who had been married solely for her money by a merry, mocking, little cynic of a multi-clubbed gentleman who was too mortally afraid of his jealous and strictly supervising spouse to indulge in the adulteries that constantly tempted him. Rosina and Elias Castor lived in a Beaux Arts house, too pompous for its exiguity, on East Seventieth Street in Manhattan and in a shingle villa in Newport. In the latter resort they clung to the fringes of the summer community that Rosina imagined that she dominated. Her husband, keener if more duplicitous, knew better.

Elihu, who had inherited a portion of his father's intelligence with his mother's fatuity, had always understood their relationship. He had seen that his mother ruled and that his father, for all his sly innuendos and somehow lewd chuckles, obeyed. He knew that their sputtering arguments always terminated in a maternal mandate and that his own soft life of ease in a household of well-trained servants depended on the emotion he aroused in the ample bosom of an adoring female parent. On evenings when she read aloud to him of the dashing rescues of the Scarlet Pimpernel he would nestle in her comfortable lap and inhale her fragrant perfume and finger her large pearls. His father's futile gibes and smutty jokes, even when he sensed in them the timid overtures of something like a paternal affection, could hardly be weighed against the conclusive power of the waved maternal wand.

But a goddess was still a goddess. He had often witnessed the effect of her wrath on others. Brunhild's *hojotoho* was a piercing cry, and if her spear was never pointed at him, it was always there. It was not hard for him to please her, but please her he must.

She wanted him constantly with her. It was she and not Nanny who picked him up after classes at Buckley, the day school he attended before Averhill; he would find her waiting for him in the luxurious back seat of the crimson Rolls-Royce where, on a cold day, she would immediately bundle him in the fur cover and hug him close. And she would take him shopping with her, asking him to advise her in choosing dresses paraded before her at Bergdorf Goodman or jewels submitted to her inspection by unctuous attendants at Tiffany's or Black, Starr & Frost. A whole room in the townhouse was devoted to the toys she bought him, including a fabulous dollhouse with period rooms furnished with objects that he and she shopped for together and carefully arranged and re-arranged.

It was this dollhouse that alerted Elihu to the existence of a world with quite other standards than Mama's and one with which he would have to learn to deal. At Buckley until he was nine, he saw little of the other boys as he went home im-mediately after classes and exercised with a private instructor in a small gymnasium room in the attic of his home. But the school persuaded the reluctant Rosina that he should be al-lowed to play ball in Central Park in the afternoon with his classmates, and he thus came to make his first friendships. One of these was with a boy called Sam Taylor, whom he made the unfortunate effort to impress by telling him of a new plan for adding a "music room" to the interior of the dollhouse. Sam chortled.

"A dollhouse! You have a dollhouse! What kind of a sissy does that make you, Castor?" He turned to the other boys. "Say, fellas, what do you know? Castor has a dollhouse!"

Poor Elihu was about to say that it was his sister's, but then he immediately realized that they would find out that he had no sister, and he said it was an old dollhouse of his mother's, but he still had to suffer gibes and pokes for some days until the incident was forgotten. He never told his mother for he had a conviction that she would not under-stand. And he never told his father for he had an intuition that he would. He thought he might give up playing with the doll's house and convince his mother that he had tired of it, but she just then had purchased a little piano for it that played a tune, and he loved it too much. It dawned on him finally that the dollhouse was a crime only at school and not at home. He did not know it, but he had made a discovery that would guide him through life. Morals were made by the environment. Silence was the answer to all.

There were plenty of occasions to develop his theory at Averhill to which he was sent at age thirteen. His going there had been a severe emotional crisis for his mother. She had hoped to keep her child at home at least until college, but she had finally been prevailed upon with the argument, presented by teachers, friends, and even her husband, that graduation from an accepted New England boarding school, was, at least in her social milieu, something of a must for social success at Harvard, Yale, or Princeton. Elias Castor had taken a rather firmer stand in this matter than in other domestic affairs; he had been briefly happy himself at Averhill, and he was far too perceptive not to see that a temporary freedom from the maternal embrace was not going to do Elihu any harm. Indeed, he may have desperately reached a hand toward the very maleness of the institution to lend him a bit of strength to oppose the overpowering opposite in his home. Yet even at that he confined his arguments in favor of the school to those that appealed to the worldly nature of his wife and her social aspirations for their son.

Visiting Averhill with Rosina after Elihu had been enrolled there, Elias, gaining confidence in the knowledge that they were now treading on his territory rather than hers, found the nerve to warn her that demanding special occasions to check on the school's services, such as insisting on a master's accompanying her on an inspection of the linen closets, covered her with a ridicule that would redound upon their son. Rosina at Averhill came the nearest to meekness she was ever to come.

The masculine note was certainly struck at Averhill. Women were only to be seen in the rather subdued and dreary faculty wives who appeared with their husbands at the ends of the long dining room tables on Sunday lunches, or in the fleeting housemaids chosen by a supervisor who employed none of even passing sex appeal. Girls, it was true, were ultimately admitted to the school before Elihu's graduation, but even then for a time they seemed to present a further hurdle to masculinity. *Did* a boy have a girlfriend? *Could* he have a girlfriend? Sports still ruled, the rougher the better: hockey, soccer, and sacred football. History and even art told the stories of great men. The tall chapel spire dominated the campus like a phallic symbol.

Yet Elihu didn't do too badly at the school. The lesson he had learned at Buckley stood him in good stead. He was comfortably in the middle of his form in grades, below the average in sports but not impossible; he respected the leaders of his group and even made a few friends among the less popular. His wish was to get by, and get by he did. One factor in his favor was the lavish parties his mother gave to his New Yorker formmates on Christmas and spring vacations, which they accepted with boyish condescension and which Elihu had the tact never to mention as entitling him to any consideration on return to school.

As the sexuality of his nature developed he began to find a pleasure in his contemplation of the handsomer boys. Members of the football team in the gymnasium showers struck him as splendid creatures, and he liked to imagine them in erotic poses or engaged in erotic acts. He was perfectly aware there were boys at Averhill who did not confine their sexual impulses to fantasy, and who engaged at night in the dormitories in different forms of sexual experiment with each other, but there seemed to be a sense, even among some of those so engaged, that it was bad, obscene, even wicked, and he was not tempted to do likewise, nor was it dangled before him, as he was not among the lovely boys whose torsos he admired. Besides, he had heard his mother once darkly refer to a departing luncheon guest as a "pervert," and his father made frequent use of such scathing terms as "fairy" or "faggot." Would that describe the boys on the squeaking bed in the adjoining cubicle? Maybe not. Maybe they were just experimenting. Elihu was a reasoning boy. But he would never join them.

For there was another feature in his picture of himself. He had learned to stand back and see the world and Elihu Castor in it. He was pretty sure that his fantasies when he masturbated, which he frequently did, were different from those of other boys. Or from the other boys at Averhill, anyway. Or, say, from the majority of the other boys at Averhill. And the majority was the group that one had at least outwardly to join. If one wasn't in the majority, at any rate, no one in the world must know it. And no one had to. That was life.

He imagined that "other boys," when they masturbated or engaged in some form of sexual activity, thought either of the dirty things they did in a cubicle with a pal or of what they did with some of the girls they met at dances on vacation, where they might rub their stiff pricks against their sometimes shocked, more often titillated partners. But Elihu had other private visions, and ones that he was quite sure were not only not shared by his classmates but which had better be kept as dark as the fatal dollhouse. He thought of himself as a girl, a goddess surprised bathing in a fountain by a peeking swain, or a nude model in the atelier of a handsome artist, or a daring beauty naked in bed with the captain of the football team. This marooned him on an island of his own. But the ferry service to the mainland was always available.

As a fourth-former, thus, at age fifteen, Elihu felt he had achieved a workable balance between his inner and outer lives. Girls had now been admitted to the school, but there were none as yet in his form, and their influence on him was nil. There was, however, in any group of schoolboys always at least one pair of eyes that could penetrate the secret of the most careful lad. "Bossy" Caldwell seemed to have been created to divine the chink in Elihu's armor the way certain foxes know how to overturn a porcupine and sink their teeth into its exposed belly. He was a big, grinning, ugly, muscular boy who would one day exercise his disgusting charm successfully on many a weak woman, but who at seventeen, and in the monastery that Averhill still essentially was, satisfied himself by playing dirty games with younger boys. As a sixth-former and a prefect with disciplinary powers in Elihu's dormitory, he scandalously misused his authority in midnight visits to the cubicles of his prey. Some boys were ready enough to oblige him, but he had a perverse inclination for the "puritans" who resisted.

He had noted Elihu's failure to join in the smutty talk with the little group of fascinated boys that surrounded the prefect at any dormitory party, like the Bandar-log around the writhing figure of the rock python Kaa, and he chose to address his lewdest remarks to him. Once he took the boy aside for a private chat.

"Ya want it, kid, don't ya?" he suggested with a leer.

"Want what, Bossy?"

"Ya know what I mean." He pressed a hand on Elihu's crotch. "I can feel it. The little Christer who's ashamed of his stiff prick."

Bossy was right. Elihu's throat was clogged with his throttled reaction.

"Go away, Bossy," he managed to murmur. "Leave me be."

Bossy gave him a swift kick in the rear and dismissed him with a mocking laugh. But that night, after lights, Bossy's large naked figure loomed in the drawn curtains of Elihu's cubicle.

"Move over, kid," he whispered. "I'm getting in."

"No, no!" Elihu hissed violently.

He struggled in vain; the arms of the much stronger boy pinned him to the bed, and he felt Bossy's fingers against his testicles. Suddenly he went limp; his body seemed to take fire; his left arm went around Bossy's neck. When orgasm came he breathed in a horrible ecstasy. After that he obeyed his partner's hissed instructions, and when Bossy, presumably satisfied, sat up, he too sat up, and, suddenly driven by an impulse, tried to kiss his assailant on the lips. He was roughly repulsed.

"Kissing is only for little fairies like you," Bossy snarled.

But as he rose from the bed to return to his own cubicle his naked outline was illuminated by a flashlight. It was the dormitory master's.

🍂 5 🍂

DAVID SMITHERS was only twenty-five and was thinking of getting a Ph.D. in literature at Yale. He had taken a job teaching English at Averhill to see if he was fitted for an academic life. Boston-bred and the son of two high school teachers, he was a very serious and conscientious young man, in love with the English romantic poets, Keats, Shelley, and Coleridge. He was gentle, even timid, but there was a strength and sincerity to his good intentions that commanded the respect of even the rowdiest boys. They sensed his essential integrity.

He had been aware for some time that the strict rule against nighttime visiting in the cubicles was being violated, for he left the door to his study open while he read late at night, but he had assumed that the patter of feet that he sometimes made out might be for some harmless need to chitchat or to exchange candy, and he thought he might safely leave the matter to the discretion of the dormitory prefect. But when he happened to mention this to a fellow master, the latter had warned him at once, and very seriously, to take steps to stop it, and it was on the night after receiving this advice that he caught Bossy in Elihu's cubicle. The prefect's nudity and the shocking violation of his duties penetrated even David's naiveté; the unhappy teacher ordered Bossy to his cubicle and retired to his study to consider for a long fretful time what he had to do. There was obviously only one course open to him, and he went the next morning, immediately after breakfast, to report the episode to the headmaster.

Michael, met at his front door on the way to morning chapel, slipped an arm under David's and listened carefully to him as they crossed the campus. He spoke not a word until they were at the chapel door, and then simply said, "Thanks, David. Send both boys to my office in the schoolhouse after chapel. And not a word about this to anyone."

But Michael's calm was all on the surface. In chapel his mind seethed. This sort of thing was a headmaster's nightmare. Disciplinary action might lead to public scandal, hurting the school; condonement might lead to worse. If only a couple of lower form boys were involved, a discreet silence after a severe warning sometimes worked; the boys themselves were terrified of their families finding out. But with a prefect implicated! If only David had shut his door!

Michael himself had spent two years in an English public school when his father had accepted an invitation to teach philosophy for that period at Oxford. He was quite aware of what had notoriously gone on among the boys in those venerable institutions in the past, some of which had subsisted to his day. He knew that to have discharged the culprits might have been to have marred the lives of some of Britain's most distinguished leaders, later the heads of fine families. And he could well imagine Bossy Caldwell as a future president of the stock exchange and the father of a dozen promising children. One had seen stranger things. And wasn't this random groping of teenage males as essentially harmless as what puppies do in a den?

He had his sixth-form class in current events, which included everything from politics to modern art, immediately after chapel, but his mind was full of the interviews that would follow it, and he found it difficult to concentrate, although the course provided him with his most fruitful contact with students. That day he had arranged to have two large pictures mounted on easels that faced the class. One was a colored reproduction of a Frederick Church painting of giant icebergs; the other, Emile Bernard's rendition of three house fronts appearing over a green park in Brittany's Pont-Aven. The subject of the day was: is either, or are both, a work of art?

The class knew its headmaster well enough by now to suspect that he would pick as his favorite what to most of them was the least attractive of the two canvases, but they were quite willing to give him a fight over it. They knew how he favored dissension.

"Those huge islands of ice enthrall me!" one girl exclaimed. "It's the kind of great picture that makes you feel how small and insignificant you are compared to mighty nature. It's exhilarating and humiliating at the same time!"

"Is that because you know how dangerous icebergs can be to navigation?" Michael asked her. "Don't you think immediately of the fate of the *Titanic*?"

"Perhaps."

"Then isn't it something outside the picture itself that sends you off? Wouldn't a perfect colored photograph have the same effect?"

"It might, but the painting's so beautiful, sir! Could a photograph ever equal it?"

"I think it's possible. With the right light and the right camera. And, like the painting, it would be a work of great beauty. That I fully concede. But is it art?"

"Why not?" a boy demanded. "If it inspires you?"

Michael at this took another look at the Church. Certainly it was more inspiring than the picture in his mind of two naked boys wriggling in a bed. Couldn't he derive a moral code from towers of ice and infinite blue water? No, he couldn't. A headmaster had other fish to fry. Scorpions rather. Why hadn't Mr. Smithers kept his damn door closed? But a prefect! A school prefect! He shook his head to scatter these intrusive thoughts.

"Because it is not the composition of the painting that arouses you," he now explained. "Whether you are actually looking at the icebergs themselves, say, from a boat, as Church himself was, or seeing them in a painting or photograph, the result to you is very much the same. It is the subject itself that does the job. Whereas if I took you to Pont-Aven and to the exact site of the houses and park in Bernard's painting, it wouldn't excite you in the least. It might even bore you. But when you look at that Bernard you are seeing something much more than three very commonplace houses and a chunk of greenery. Those bus rides in Provence that take you to the sites where Cézanne painted are perfectly ridiculous. The whole point is what artists like Cézanne and Bernard *did* with what they saw. It is their vision of the ordinary that is interesting. Or even exciting."

"Why is it exciting?" another boy, with a touch of truculence, wanted to know. "What is it that Bernard is trying to tell me? I don't get it at all. Am I just another hopeless philistine, sir?"

"It doesn't matter what you are, Billy. What matters is that you are reacting to a work of art very differently from the way you reacted to the icebergs. That is a beginning in the process of appreciation. You will soon begin to see other things in those houses. Is the artist doing something with the contrast between their banal regularity and the seeming disorganization of the chunks of greenery below them? But look again. Isn't there actually a more interesting organization in the squares and triangles of the leaves? Why do the three different colors of the house fronts meld with the total greenness of the park in such a way as to create a startling beauty? Doesn't Bernard make beauty out of nothing, so to speak, while Church simply reproduces it?"

He saw that he was not getting through to the class, and that they were now confining their opposition to silence. After all, he *was* the headmaster, and they were not going to tell him that he was all wet. Besides they liked him well enough and didn't give a damn if he preferred a Bernard they had never heard of to the celebrated Church. Grownups were apt to be a bit wacky, but they had to be tolerated.

He decided that he was in no mood to go on with his theorizing about art, and stepping to a closet he brought out a large reproduction of Picasso's *Les Demoiselles d'Avignon* and propped it up before the class, explaining, for the benefit of those who mightn't know, that the five women depicted were prostitutes in a brothel. He then directed them to use the remainder of the hour writing down any thoughts that the painting evoked in them.

He now took out of his briefcase to reread a piece that Bossy Caldwell had submitted some months before to the school magazine and which Michael, using the veto power of the headmaster over all contributions, had refused to approve, on the grounds that it might seriously upset some of the more religiously devout of the parent body and cause them to fear that their loved ones were being sadly misled at Averhill. Caldwell, under questioning, had been rather impertinently casual about this censorship, and Michael had pulled the piece from his files to reexamine it and gain some further insight into the boy's character. It purported to be a sermon by a staunch right-winger priest and started as follows:

> My subject this morning is taken from the fourth chapter of the book of Ezekiel where it is related that the Lord God issued this command to the prophet: that he should go to the rebellious children of Israel and endure the iniquity of the House of Judah for forty days and eat their

bread as barley cakes and bake it with dung that cometh out of man in their sight. But when Ezekiel protested that he had never eaten abominable flesh, the Lord in his mercy mitigated the rigor of his command by substituting the dung of cows for that of man. Blessed be the name of the Lord!

Michael had originally been amused by this piece and had rather regretted having to ban it. He hoped that the boy's teenage malevolent joy in smashing the idols in the Christian temple would be tempered in time in such a way as to turn him into a more moderate and thus more effective critic of the establishment. He hated the idea of throwing out of the school any student whose faults he deemed it his duty to correct. Where was the fame in graduating boys and girls who were already stars? Couldn't anyone do that?

But Caldwell was a prefect of the school—that was the rub. If he were forgiven this episode wouldn't critics have some justification in saying that Michael was turning the school into a reformatory? This even brought him to think back on his days as a journalist with something like nostalgia. What bliss to be able simply to report and not to have to punish! Was he too soft for the task he had undertaken?

Bossy Caldwell was waiting in his office when Michael came down from his classroom. Like a juvenile defendant clad by a jury-conscious lawyer, he was wearing a newly pressed black suit and a sober blue tie. His rather craggy features and stocky build seemed unaccustomed to his conservative apparel, and Michael thought he could detect the ghost of a sneer under the blandly attentive face that confronted him. It would be at least interesting to see how he would defend himself.

Michael silently took the seat behind his desk and motioned to Caldwell to take the chair opposite. A silence ensued.

"Well, Caldwell?"

"Well, what, sir?"

"I'm waiting to hear you explain what you were doing in Elihu Castor's cubicle last night."

Caldwell suddenly demonstrated an actual eagerness to get to the point. "I've had some hours to think this over, and when you're in a real jam, I guess the best ploy is to be utterly frank. You have the reputation, sir, of being a fair and impartial judge, a man one can really talk to, and I'm going to put all my cards on the table."

There was a note of near impertinence in this effort to reduce the gulf between them to that of man to man, but Michael chose to ignore it.

"By all means do so."

"If I may take the liberty, sir, I'd like to observe that you are believed to take a wider and more realistic view of these matters than many other New England heads."

"What matters?"

"Well, sir, it's well known that you attended a boarding school in England. You must have observed what sometimes goes on between unsupervised boys."

"We're going to leave out of this discussion, Caldwell, any things that I may or may not have observed in the United Kingdom or elsewhere." Michael's tone was stern. "We are going to confine it to you."

"Very well, sir. Excuse me, sir. But in my own defense, I'm going to have to tell you what *I* have observed going on in my dormitory at night."

"That's all right. Go ahead."

"As a prefect in my dormitory I had to take account of the plain fact that there was a certain amount of intervisiting in the cubicles after lights. And it wasn't to play tiddlywinks, either."

"Never mind what it wasn't, Caldwell. I'm perfectly aware of what it was. There's no place for humor in this discussion. It was your clear duty as prefect to put a stop to any visiting at all. How did you implement that duty?"

"I would warn any culprit I apprehended that if he was caught again, I would report him to Mr. Smithers."

"But Mr. Smithers tells me you never reported anyone. Do you mean to imply that there were no repeats among the boys you so warned?"

"No, sir. I have to confess that when it came to actually reporting a boy, the soft side of my nature got the better of me. I couldn't bear to be responsible for some poor kid maybe being kicked out of school for doing something his natural urges impelled him to do."

Michael noted the attempted shift of the argument to a case of civil rights. "Which brings us then, Caldwell, to a consideration of your own 'natural urges.' Was it one of these that induced you to enter Castor's cubicle?"

"No, sir, not in entering it, anyway. To explain what happened *after* I had entered it requires further explanation."

"Let us hear it."

"The Castor boy was the victim of what the girls call a crush on me. A better term for boys would be 'the hots.' He would follow me into the showers and stare at my you-know-what. He was always making up excuses for consulting me about dormitory regulations or laundry or whatnot. Anything to get himself into my attention. Of course, I saw what his trouble was, and I felt sorry for the kid and tried to be as nice to him as I could, but he bored me. And then one night he actually came into my cubicle after lights and started sobbing and told me he couldn't get back to sleep, that he'd had the most terrifying nightmare, that he was worried sick about his mother who was having a test for cancer, and would I please, please, come and sit with him a moment until he got hold of himself."

"Which you did?"

"Which I did, sir. The kid was in a state. I thought it wouldn't hurt if I put him back to bed and even gave him a hug to help put him to sleep."

"And was it necessary for you to be naked while administering this consolation?"

"I never use pajamas, sir. I was bareass when Castor came in. Excuse the term, sir. It slipped out."

Michael was not sure it had just slipped out, but he ignored this. "And did you hug the boy?" Caldwell nodded. "And do you maintain that nothing else happened after that?"

"No, sir, I don't," he replied stoutly. "Castor went kind of crazy when I bent down over his bed to embrace him. He threw his arms around my neck. He reached down to grab my balls. He tried to kiss them. I'm sorry, sir, but I've got to be explicit. There's too much at stake for me in this. You have to see it as it was. I was aroused, yes. What man wouldn't be? I'm only human. I fucked the hell out of the kid. And did he love it!"

Michael stared down at the blotter on his desk for a long moment. If it wasn't the whole truth, Caldwell at least was an able actor.

"You've been frank with me, Caldwell. At least I hope you have. And I'll be frank with you. I do not regard consensual sexual acts between boys in the same lurid light that some teachers do. But I agree it is better for the young to abstain until they reach an age when they may have a more mature recognition of their basic sexual orientation, and for this reason nightly visitation in the dorms is strictly forbidden. Your taking advantage of a younger boy may be somewhat mitigated by his aggressive behavior, but you had no business being in his cubicle at all. If he really needed help, you should have gone to Mr. Smithers, and he could have taken the boy to the infirmary."

"Oh, I plead guilty to that, sir!" Caldwell affirmed, almost with enthusiasm, as if snatching at a lesser penalty. "It was a gross violation of my duty as a prefect, and if you kick me out of your school, I can hardly complain!"

Was this the smartest ploy of all? Michael sighed as he dismissed the culprit, telling him that his case would be duly considered. What he didn't quite like was the boy's insinuation that, after all, he and the headmaster were of the same breed of sophisticated men of the world who understood the imperative call of nature in such matters, for all their having to give lip service to the hypocritical priests of a supposedly Christian society. Had his school reforms given rise to the suspicions in boys like Caldwell that he had no morals at all?

Very different was his interview with Elihu Castor. The boy was pale and visibly shaken. He listened, intently staring at his interlocutor while Michael delivered this gentle lecture.

"Elihu, I want to start by telling you that there is nothing to be deeply ashamed about if you find yourself developing a strong affection for an older boy. It is a perfectly natural thing, and I well remember when I was at Harrow in England feeling the greatest admiration for the captain of my house's cricket team. The mutual admiration of a young warrior and an older one was applauded in classical times. But these affections can sometimes be carried too far and result in physical relationships. This is not a good idea, for the higher-minded among us feel that love should not be coupled with sexual acts until a man has attained his full maturity and has a better knowledge of what he really needs. Do you get what I mean, Elihu?"

"You mean that Bossy Caldwell should have waited to see what he really needs?"

"Yes, in a way." Michael was a bit taken aback. "Both of you, for that matter. Caldwell is older, of course. He probably already is more attracted to girls than he is to boys like you."

"You mean he was attracted to *me?*"

"Well, wasn't he?"

"He didn't act that way."

"Is the idea so impossible?"

Whatever the idea was, it suddenly seemed to intrigue the boy, for it actually appeared to distract him from the trouble he was in. Did he like to play with the concept that he, poor little thing that he was, had aroused something in the heart of the big brute of a prefect? A David subduing Goliath?

"But he was always nasty to me," he muttered in a sudden reversal of mood. "He even called me a fairy."

"He was probably ashamed of what he had done with you. Some men are like that. It's a way of reasserting their masculinity by blaming their partner for what happened."

"But even Bossy could hardly blame me for that, sir."

"Why not? Didn't you entice him into your cubicle?"

"No! He came into my cubicle and grabbed me! He did it all! He pinned me down!"

Michael became very grave at this. "You didn't resist him?"

"How could I? He's too big and strong."

"You could have cried out. The dormitory master's open door was only a few yards away."

"Bossy would have killed me! You don't know him, sir!"

Michael thought for a minute. The sheets on Elihu's bed had been stained; David Smithers had had the housemaid's report after chapel. Was it usual for the victim of an assault to achieve orgasm? Of course the sperm might have been Bossy's alone. Would Elihu think of that? Michael became inquisitorial.

"But you both reached a climax, didn't you?"

"Sir, he manipulated me!"

Michael thought now that he knew what had happened. The boy had enjoyed himself and was in terror of being found out. Little did he care what damage he did to Bossy. The instant dislike that he felt for the whining and falsely accusing Elihu promoted a reluctant sympathy with the lustful but truthful Bossy. Maybe there was a way that this whole nasty business could be made to go away. He remembered the odious Mrs. Castor.

"You know, Elihu, if you persist in accusing Caldwell, this whole thing will become public. You're not anxious to have your mother brought into this, are you?"

"Oh no, sir! Oh, not at all!"

"Suppose we keep it just between ourselves and Mr. Smithers? I can promise you that Caldwell will never bother you again. He's thoroughly sorry for what he did. Sex is a funny thing, Elihu, and it sometimes gets out of hand. If Caldwell did what he did to you entirely against your will, he is bound to be expelled from school. You don't want that to happen, do you?"

"No, sir. But it wouldn't be my fault, would it?"

"Not if you're telling me the absolute truth, no. But are you, Elihu? We all know these things are capable of subtle gradations. There can be reluctance and resistance and acquiescence all mixed up together. I've watched lions mating in Kenya. The females sometimes bite and scratch the males before giving in." Michael feared he might be going too far, but he had to get to the truth.

"But if it wasn't entirely against my will, mightn't I be thrown out too?"

Ah, there it was! *That* was the reason for the boy's charge of rape. Michael breathed in relief. "Elihu," he said seriously, "I give you my word as headmaster that whether you resisted or failed to resist you will not be subjected to any disciplinary action. You did not leave your cubicle except to appeal to the prefect about feeling ill, which is perfectly allowable. And when another boy improperly enters your cubicle and climbs into your bed, you are not held responsible for what follows. So no matter what your testimony about Caldwell amounts to, you are in the clear. And now I repeat, are you one hundred percent sure that you in no way cooperated with Caldwell in what happened that night? That it was, from start to finish, entirely against your will?"

A long pause ensued. "No, sir, I'm not," the boy at last confessed.

"Thank you, Elihu. That will be all."

Michael hoped he had finally disposed of the matter when he relieved Caldwell of his prefectship, assigned him to another dormitory, and gave him thirty hours of weekend tasks, clearing snow off faculty driveways and washing their cars. To Elihu nothing was done.

But he was surprised, when he described the case to Ione one night, that she did not wholly approve of his action.

"Did you ask the Castor boy if he had told Caldwell of his mother's cancer scare?"

"No. It was an obvious bid for sympathy."

"But did the boy actually use it?"

"I assumed so."

"That might have been the key. You should learn to be more suspicious, my dear. It would stand you in good stead if you ever found yourself in the position of a foundation head having to give away large sums of money."

"Now what in the world made you think of that?"

"Something I've been waiting all day to tell you. I've a letter from the chairman of the Gladwin Foundation asking me if you were interested enough in their directorship to come down to New York for a preliminary interview."

He gave her a long hard stare. "Ione, what have you been up to?"

"I simply told him at the wedding anniversary party that you were well qualified for the job. He was the one who brought the matter up. I didn't commit you in any way. I didn't even say you were interested."

"I'm not. But obviously you are. That's what troubles

me. Oh, my poor darling, are you so wretched at Averhill?"

"No, no! I'm only thinking of you and your future. Really, I am! Won't you go down, even for just an interview?"

"I could not think of leaving the school at this juncture. Even for you, my dearest!"

"Oh, I'd hate it if you did it only for me!" And to his dismay, she burst into tears. "Oh, we'll stay in Averhill forever, of course. For ever and ever! And I'm going to be good about it, too. I mean that!"

Michael did the only thing he could do: he made love to her. But he was beginning to wonder if he might be becoming a bit of a Bossy Caldwell. As Bossy Caldwell seemed already to suspect.

❧ 6 ❧

MICHAEL AFTERWARD always told himself that it might have worked. The thing that wrecked it was something he could never have guessed and something to which the answer was never found. How did Bossy find out that Elihu had accused him of rape? Had he simply divined it from the fact that no disciplinary action was taken? Was he subtle enough to have gleaned the fact that no headmaster could afford the publicity that such an accusation would arouse? He was certainly very subtle.

It later appeared that Caldwell had snarled at Elihu, "I'm going to get you for what you did, you little fairy sneak. You won't know when or how until it happens, but you'll know every minute of the day and night it's surely coming! Oh, yes, we'll get you!"

"We," poor Elihu wondered. Who were "we"? Perhaps the whole mighty sixth form, uniting to avenge one of their own? Would they "pump" him, as the terrible term was, for a revenge carried out while a sympathetic faculty turned its back? Mightn't they even drown him by mistake?

Elihu lived now in such panic that he could hardly concentrate on his studies. In his dormitory the boys didn't know just what had happened on the night when Mr. Smithers had found Bossy Caldwell in his cubicle and sent him sharply back to his own, but the speculation was rife and lewd. What they did surmise from Bossy's sly wink and shoulder shrug and malevolent glance at Elihu was that the latter had been guilty of some dishonorable "snitch" for which nemesis was waiting. In a matter of only a week Elihu was assigned to the infirmary with some kind of undiagnosed nervous disorder, and the next his dormmates knew was that he had been sent home for an indefinite period to effect a cure.

Elihu's panic dissolved behind the thick walls of the protecting Beaux Arts mansion on Seventieth Street, but he knew that his salvation depended on his never returning to Averhill, at least while Bossy was there. There was obviously only one way to assure himself of this, and at last he gathered the courage to tell his story to his anxious mother, who had had him under constant interrogation as to just what had occurred at school to upset him so. In his version of the episode, of course, Bossy appeared as a lustful ape and himself as the chaste and violated victim.

The result was even more than he had hoped. His mother's eyes widened as he had never seen them do, and her scream tore his eardrums.

"Oh, my poor darling ravished child! What can I do to make up for this dreadful thing? Tell me, tell me, my sweety boy, what Mama can do to console you and make you happy again and safe again and her own lovey-dovey innocent babe?" With which she almost smothered him in a maternal hug.

"Don't send me back there, please Mummy. Don't send me back."

"Send you back! To that den of iniquity! I should think not. I'll send something back to that cesspool—you can be sure of that—but it won't be my darling boy."

Asking him now what he would like to do, of all the wonderful things she could offer him to take his mind off the horror, she was a trifle surprised at the speed with which he announced his desire to go to a popular musical comedy, but he was sent off to it at a matinée that same day while she went at once to her lawyer's office.

That night, when her husband came home from his afternoon bridge game at his club, she told the butler to ask him to meet her in the library. When Elias came in she told him solemnly to close the door behind him.

"What's up?" he asked, as he complied. "Has your new maid mixed up your winter underwear with your summer things? Oh, but that was last week, wasn't it?"

"You like to be funny, Elias, about everything, but today I won't have it. Our son has been subject to a horrible experience at school. Another boy, a school prefect, invaded his cubicle at night."

"Oh, that sort of thing still goes on, does it? It did in my day, but I rather thought they'd cleaned it up."

Rosina had been sitting but now she rose and loomed before him. "Elias Castor, our child has been raped! Do you understand what I am saying?"

He knew at once he had to look serious. He was well aware when Rosina was dangerous, and when she was dangerous she could be very much so. He came forward now and took a seat, indicating that she should also do so. "Forgive my silly tongue, Rosina, and tell me all about it."

It was obviously not going to be one of those moments, like too many others in the minor crises of his largely untroubled life, when he could count on laughs to get him through. These had been his sole refuge in the existence that had preceded his married life, when he had lived with his family, scions of "old New York," as serious as they were high-minded, but of more lineage than cash, with a brilliant lawyer father who had died young before his fortune was realized, a heroic mother who had somehow made ends meet, and two older brothers who had been Phi Beta Kappas and athletic stars at Yale. Elias, far the youngest and certainly the least talented, blond, short, easygoing, cynical, sensual, and always joking, had from childhood refused to compete with the lofty family standards in morals and games and studies, turning a good-natured back on the disapproval of his siblings and ultimately changing the ill will of his surrounding society into a grudging respect for his bubbling wit and unrebuffable good nature. His favorite motto was Oscar Wilde's famous advice on how to deal with temptation, and he dared cheerfully to proclaim to all that it was his inexorable fate—thank you very much—to marry for money. Which at age thirty he did. And no one who met Rosina was under any illusion that he could have had any other motive.

There had, however, been one serious period in his unserious life, and it unfolded now before him as his wife inveighed against the horror of Averhill. At age sixteen he had been briefly happy at that school. His ebullient nature and cheerful humor had gained him a mild but definite popularity even with the more athletic leaders of the form, and he had found a resource in poetry that had actually turned his mind away from himself. And he had formed a close friendship with Tommy Bendle, who later became a recognized poet. The two of them had taken long weekend hikes in the beautiful autumnal countryside, reciting quatrains from the *Rubáiyat*. Elias had even composed a dramatic monologue in what he hoped was the style of Browning about the apostacy of the Roman emperor Julian. It had been a heady time, and he had known a new happiness, but at Yale, where both boys matriculated, Elias was lured too often to New York for debutante parties, and Bendle, increasingly immersed in his verse making, had become something of a recluse. The friendship drooped and finally ended when Elias chose another roommate more in the social swing of college life.

It was the nostalgic memory of those halcyon Averhill days, shedding a roseate glow over the past, that now jarred disagreeably with Rosina's hysterical denunciations.

"Please, please, Rosina," he pleaded, "can't you take this a little more calmly? Let us go over it step by step. Surely you are not implying that the school does not thoroughly disapprove of what Elihu says happened to him?"

"What Elihu *says!*" Rosina almost shrieked. "Do you think our son would lie?"

"Any boy might lie."

"But not about a thing like this! You don't seem to realize that the child was violated."

Patiently he listened to her repetition of the episode. A very similar thing had happened to him at Averhill, and he recalled it with unblushing pleasure. It had started with his being rather pushed around, but that was not the way it had ended. Had something of the same sort happened to Elihu? Possibly. But even if not, what harm was done? Boys did that sort of thing. Elihu might well be in emotional trouble, but that was not from Averhill. His mother had been the cause of that.

"Very well," he said at last. "I think I get the picture. What I fail to see is what you expect us to do about it. If we raise a stink, do you think that is going to help our boy when he goes back to the school?"

"Elias Castor, what are you talking about? Do you think I'm ever going to return my son to that sink of perversion? Never in your life! You ask what I'm going to do about it. I'm going to give that institution the treatment it deserves. I'm going to prosecute it! I'm going to sue it! I'm going to blacken its name from coast to coast!"

"You want damages?"

"I want justice!"

"You don't care then that this sort of publicity may redound badly on Elihu?"

"Why should it? He's innocent, the poor boy. He's the victim. He will grow up to understand that there are cases where a decent citizen must brave dirt thrown to expose crime!"

"A crime? How has the school broken a law?"

"By failing to report Elihu's complaint. There's a Massachusetts statute that requires the school to inform the local DA of any student's allegation of a sexual assault. This was obviously not done. The whole thing was hushed up."

"You've talked to a lawyer already, Rosina?"

"Damn right I have!"

"I think you might have told me first."

Rosina exploded at this. "Why should I have done that? When have you been the slightest help to me in any of my legal or financial affairs? Have you done anything but be the recipient of my bounty? Well, I'm telling you right now, Elias Castor, that I am expecting some small return for all that I've done for you since our marriage. I don't half like your attitude in this matter. You don't seem to care about what your own son has miserably suffered. I want you to stand behind me in every step I take in this business, and if you fail me there are plenty of ways in which I can fail you. Don't put me to it. I made one mistake in letting you talk me into sending the boy to this filthy school. I don't intend to make another."

She had risen and was standing before him in a threatening pose, her thick rouged lips flapping as she spoke, her dyed red head shaking. He thought of Jezebel and how she had been thrown down from a high window and consumed by dogs. But he felt a sickness in his stomach with the realization of his utter impotence. Unknown to her his gambling debts at one of his clubs had risen to twenty thousand dollars, and he would need all his diminishing credit with her to get them paid.

7

HUDDLED AT THE TIP of a small rocky peninsula, sticking its nose into the rough Atlantic off Cape Cod, was a dark, weather-beaten pile of shingle surrounded by deep porches and surmounted by inexplicable towers, the summer residence of Ezra Prentice, retired senior partner of Prentice & Brooks, one of State Street's most venerable law firms. And seated on the porch with the veteran jurist, contemplating a sea preparing itself for an early spring storm, was his son, Hiram, the small, balding, pale but aspiring district attorney from a mid-state county. Both held in their hands dark glasses of undiluted whiskey.

"There's very little point in your coming to see me, Hiram, if you don't take my advice." Ezra's tone was emphasized by a deep crackle. "You can do as I say, and maybe one day be governor of the state. Who knows? Stranger things have happened. Or you can listen to that mollycoddle of a wife of yours and end up precisely where you started."

"But, Father, I never said I wasn't going to take your advice," the son protested. "I was just asking you to look at the question from some other points of view."

"It's the same damn thing."

"Is it? You think I'm going against you when I point out that scandals about sex have sometimes boomeranged against the politicians who have used them?"

"Against the politicians who have misused them! You've got a clear case, my boy."

"How can I be sure of that?"

"Because it's the kind of flung dung that always sticks. Now you listen to me, Hiram, while I go over a few fundamentals of who we are, men like you and me, and how we got to where we've got. *I* know it's an old story, but something tells me that your memory needs jogging. It's probably the fault of that wife of yours. A man who mixes his wife with his business is a man lost."

Ezra Prentice looked the part he had played in American life as if he had been painted by Grant Wood. His big body and long face were rough and gnarled, as weather-beaten as his summer villa; his beetling brow, steely gray hair, and eagle's nose might have been the prow of an old whaler headed into a giant billow. He ran a small summer fishing business around his peninsula and helped the hired men to haul in the nets in the early morning. Hairs protruded from his ears and nostrils.

"People think we're a type that has died out, but we're a lot tougher than that. We've had to move over a bit to make room for the decadent hordes, but we're still here. We learned with John Winthrop that a New England winter had to be coped with and that a good Indian was a dead

Indian. And we're not going to be put off by all the crazy modern isms-makers that have invaded the land: the Irish mackerel snatchers, the socialists and commies, and all the deluded do-gooders who would make hash of our state. They can be controlled, but to be controlled they have to be watched. They have to be manipulated! They have to be understood."

"But, Father, I know all that. How does it help me with this Averhill case?"

"That's what I'm coming to if you'll just hold your horses. Averhill is another of these rich New York–supported nests of liberal thought to which all the pinko teachers whose heroes we've defeated at the polls have retreated to bide their time. Half the universities and private schools in the nation fall into that category. And you, my son, are offered a double-edged sword! Not only can you deliver a fatal blow to a sick academy, you can achieve public acclaim from a moral majority that still honors a few decent principles. Or thinks it does."

"But what happened to this Castor kid might have happened in any other school. You know that, Dad. Is it fair to single out Averhill to be the scapegoat for what goes on everywhere?"

"Hiram, do you want to go places in politics or don't you?"

"Of course I do, but a man should still have some principles, shouldn't he? You were just mentioning them yourself."

"Yes, but not when you have a chance like this one. Of course, I know what boys do, and I don't give a damn about it, either. That's not the point. The point is that sex is a weapon that every politician on his toes must know how and when to use. It's a kind of atomic bomb that you have to be careful with, but there are times when it's indispensable. Schools today are dominated by the mothers who don't know beans about what their little darlings are up to. You can terrify them with words like *sodomy*, or *buggery*, or *oral sex*, or *rape*. By God, this case could make you governor!"

"You make it sound as if it were a kind of moral duty."

"Well, call it that if you like! Haven't I heard that Averhill is bowing to the general trend and is going to admit girls?"

"Oh, it just has."

"Then there you are. The school will become a brothel! Tell the mothers: Send your innocent young daughter to Averhill, and she'll be raped like the Castor boy!"

8

WILLY WELDON, the senior master and head of the clas-
sics department, a stout, fussy fiftiesh bachelor with a round
puffy face and grayish hair parted in the middle, was listen-
ing to the chairman of the trustees over an excellent lunch in
Boston's Ritz Hotel. At the school people were apt to listen
to Willy, who could charm both students and faculty with his
purring wit and love of gossip but who could also command
immediate respect when the purr suddenly swelled into
a stentorian burst of temper. But Willy would never show
the latter to the few he acknowledged to be his superiors, of
whom Donald Spencer was certainly one, and the fine Latin
scholar, the editor of a nationally used textbook on Virgil
and Horace, was now offering an attention to the chairman
that was almost reverential.

"It's important to me, Weldon," Spencer was saying,
"that you be up to date on all that is unfolding in this case.
Before I recommend any action to the board, I shall need
the support of some of the older faculty members who have
been out of sympathy with the drastic changes inaugurated

in the last few years. You know, of course, that the Castors are demanding not only a half million in damages, but a full apology. What you don't know as yet is that the trustees in yesterday's meeting voted to reject their demands in toto. There were some who wanted to leave the door open for a possible settlement, but the vote denying the apology was unanimous. The Castors' counsel can be expected to file the complaint in court no later than next week, so we're in for it."

Willy's eyes glistened. Mightn't the very fact that Spencer had arranged their meeting outside the school signify that he felt a delicacy about taking any action against the headmaster on the campus itself? Had the golden moment really come when Sayre could be compelled to resign? For two years now he had been in constant veiled communication with the chairman, who had easily gleaned the abhorrence of the Latin scholar for a schedule that rendered the dead languages optional and of the confirmed and virtuous old bachelor for the introduction of chattering, giggling girls to what he had deemed a kind of monastery. Willy had naturally apprehended that he himself would appear in this new academy, where youth was so blithely catered to, as an old fogy, a relic of an era that had been rightly consigned to the dustbin. In such a situation was rebellion not sanctified? Willy had been passionately loyal to Michael's predecessor, the Reverend Paul Prideaux, who for forty years had dominated the school with his fervent Episcopalian oratory, his faith in the ordered life, and his command presence. And he had tried his best to be similarly loyal to Michael at first, but there had come a time when he had had to decide that some sort of resistance was needed to save the life work of Dr. Prideaux from total annihilation. But until this lunch he had not thought it feasible actually to oust the headmaster.

"And it's not only the Castors' suit," Spencer continued. "Our lawyer has also informed me that the state of Massachusetts is about to bring criminal proceedings against the school for not reporting to it the Castor boy's complaint, as required by statute. Is it not now actually the duty of the chairman of the school trustees to institute an inquiry as to the fitness to continue in office of a headmaster whose action—or nonaction—has brought this obloquy down on our heads? What do you say to that, Weldon? Eh?"

"Dear me, sir, I suppose it may be."

"You just suppose? You don't roundly affirm it?"

Willy quailed, as before a basilisk. "Yes, sir, I affirm it."

He trembled a bit as he spoke. Strongly as he felt, he had never expected to be compelled to choose sides openly in a conflict that might prove an ugly one to win and an uglier one to lose. Only as late as the previous summer had he come to realize the almost sinister power that Spencer exercised over those who came within his sphere of influence. Willy, who enjoyed a small inherited trust income in addition to his salary, had been able to rent a suite for the summer months in a plush hotel in Bar Harbor, Maine, where he was pleasantly entertained in the great houses of hostesses delighted to find so cultivated an extra man for their dinner parties.

But he had recently found that, in the month when Spencer occupied the great Stone mansion on the Shore Path that his father had left to him, he was monopolized by the chairman, who wanted exhaustively to know everything that had gone on in Averhill in the previous year.

"Affirmation may not be quite enough, my friend," the remorseless Spencer now went on. "I want to know if I can expect your active cooperation in this matter."

"But isn't it, sir, a matter for the board? Would they really wish to have the faculty involved?"

"Shouldn't they? Look here, Weldon. If Michael Sayre finds there's a movement to unseat him, he's going to fight it, and fight hard. He's not the type to go quietly. I've known him most of my life, and you can believe me when I tell you that. There'll be a war and a bloody one, and not one in which innocent bystanders are spared. Everyone will be involved whether they like it or not: trustees, faculty, alumni, parents, even the students. I want to know, Weldon, just how you stand. And whether you'll help me or not."

Willy glanced nervously at those small staring eyes. The yellow in them seemed even yellower.

"Oh, I'm with you, of course, sir."

"I thought if nothing else would bring you around, your moral sense would. I can't imagine William Weldon tolerating open sex on Averhill's campus. Girls with boys. Boys with boys. Girls with girls. And, eventually, even with faculty members. Why not? A free-for-all. The great Michael has no vulgar prejudices!"

Willy stiffened at last. His beloved Averhill had always been, at least in its ideals, a citadel of virtue where the carnal appetites of the world were kept outside firmly closed gates. It was a stalwart monastery free from designing, undulating, lewd women and giggling, perverted males. Not that the inmates were monks. Far from it. They were more like King Arthur's knights—strong, chivalric, pure—who would remain unstained until they met their virgin mates—*after* and not before their graduation.

"Oh, yes, I'm with you, Mr. Spencer!" he gasped.

"But I want more than that," the inexorable chairman continued. "I want to know that you'll work with me if I undertake this thing. You have given me the names already of those on the faculty who are opposed, or at least lukewarm, to the headmaster's innovations. I want to know which we can count on to support me when it comes to their being interrogated, as they will be, by trustees and alumni."

"Yes, sir." Willy sighed.

"Good. I've brought a faculty list. Let's go over it, one by one."

Which they did, over a very good meal that Willy was hardly able to relish.

He had loved Averhill from his own school days there. As a boy he had been a great deal stouter than he now was—almost freakish—until a doctor, fearing the weight on his heart, had dieted him for a year, reducing him to a more normal if still chubby appearance. The early condition had seemed an objection to his being sent away to school, at least to his mother, a plain, dowdy, goodhearted, over-dressed rattle of a woman who uncritically adored the sole issue of her old loins, but not to his dry stick of a father, the tall, grim, and usually silent light of the Boston municipal bond bar, who insisted that a Beacon Street Weldon must go to Averhill.

Of course, he was called "Fatty" by the boys, but his brilliance in Latin and Greek, his funny jokes and friendly smiles, aroused a mild respect, and his appalling screams of fury if attacked, plus the fact that his physical condition seemed to make violence bad form, protected him from the usual hazing. And after his excess avoirdupois was shed, he achieved an actual popularity as a campus figure. He had found his niche and was completely happy.

The conviction that he had, quite passively and unresentfully, acquired as an obese boy—that he could never be attractive to girls—unfortunately survived into his normalcy. In adulthood he enjoyed the company of women—he always loved chitchat and gossip—but his friendships with the opposite sex tended to be with those whose age or plainness had taken them out of the field of gallantry or had at least rendered them more open to platonic pleasures. As sex seemed to be closed to him, it was natural for him to denigrate it, and this denigration with the passage of years slowly slipped into sourness and finally disgust. Women who indulged in it save in wedlock were sluts or whores; men, satyrs; lovers of their own sex, dykes or faggots.

A principal blessing of Averhill, of course, was that, at

least under the Reverend Prideaux's stern aegis, sex had no recognized place on the campus. Chastity reigned; law and order prevailed; the dead languages flourished. Graduating from Harvard, a much less exalted institution, Willy applied for a post on the Averhill faculty where he was warmly greeted, as competent teachers of Latin and Greek were not easy to find, and as Prideaux liked to have under him masters he had himself trained and whom he could fully trust. And as Willy had a sharp eye for everything that went on at a school he cherished and rarely left, and possessed the ability to inspire students in his classes, amuse them in his dormitory, and awe them into obedience with his soaring temper, his rise in the hierarchy was steady until he reached the post of senior master, directly under the head. The students attributed to him a kind of second sight; he seemed to sniff out infractions of the rules before they happened. Yet there was respect, even a grudging affection, in their attitude. He liked the boys, and it was considered a privilege by them to be invited on an evening after study hour to gather in his great book-lined study and listen to his fine collection of classical records, or even gossip about the day's events on the campus, for Willy could become quite cozily confidential with his favorites.

His mother, who had finally given up her long cherished sentimental hope of seeing her "darling Willy" take a lovely young bride, decided, after her somber husband's death, that it had to be up to her to supply her son with a mate—herself. For a lady of her fatuity she showed a surprising subtlety: she purchased a house not so near the school as to suggest that she was pushing herself into her son's life but close enough to provide easy access to him whenever he wished relief from the academic routine and to give him a place in which to entertain his friends on the faculty or in the neighborhood. She was shrewd enough to perceive that the masters at Averhill had little opportunity to enjoy blue-ribbon cooking and the finest French wines, and she soon became a popular figure with them and their wives, whose names and family problems she was careful to learn. Willy, who loved her as dearly as he had not his unsympathetic father, rejoiced in her presence and in her discretion. She only once had the courage to offer him a piece of advice—unwelcome as advice usually is—and that was at her end, when she was dying of cancer, and he was sitting, tearful and distraught, at her bedside.

"Forgive me for saying it, dear son, but I haven't been able to avoid noticing in the past year that the differences between your ideas and the headmaster's seem to be sharpening."

"I'm afraid that's so. With some of the older masters I tender a perhaps vain hope that we may ultimately effect some kind of restraint on him."

"Oh, my darling, I hope you keep that just as advice."

Willy was a bit startled. "What do you mean?"

"Well, you know that Mr. Sayre did me the honor of placing me on his right at the school birthday dinner."

"And no more than was your due."

"That's as it may be. But he made a reference to your opposition to some of his changes. He was humorous and charming as he always is, but I got the distinct impression that he was giving me a warning that he wanted me to pass on to you."

"A warning?" Willy felt the rumblings in his chest that usually preceded one of his outbursts. "A warning about what?"

"Not to carry things too far. Not to organize the faculty against him, perhaps."

"He has his nerve!"

"Oh, dear one, please! Be careful!"

Willy couldn't go on with it, for the excitement was clearly too much for her. He kissed her and sent the nurse in. That night she passed into a coma, and three days later she died.

He was shocked at how much he missed her. He had always been gratefully aware of the bond that united them, but he found that it was even stronger than he had supposed. In the year that ensued his temper became worse, and he even caught himself irrationally connecting her demise with the headmaster's misfeasance. He had been in the habit of holding monthly conferences between himself and three other masters who shared his hostility to Sayre to discuss the changes at the school, and now, after his Ritz luncheon with Spencer, he increased these meetings to once a week. Spencer was demanding action, and Willy desperately needed advice. Action, at least other than as executive officer, had never been his forte. He had not been made to be a ship's captain.

Tim Giles, the hirsute and excitable forty-year-old history teacher and junior member of what he didn't hesitate to call a cabal, had no such inhibitions.

"If in addition to this Castor suit," he exclaimed, "we had an instance of tolerated or deliberately ignored sodomy on the campus, mightn't it blow the ground from under Sayre? He might survive one filthy case, but could he survive two?"

"What are you suggesting, Tim?" Willy asked.

"Well, take our chaplain. Everyone knows he's gay, but he's supposed never to *do* anything about it. So far as we can see, anyway. But he's very cozy with Sayre's new male secretary—Schultze's assistant—what's his name? Andrews. I know they've been to Boston together a couple of times, presumably for a matinee. Presumably. Who knows what they do when they're alone in the Hub?"

"And what can we make of that, Tim?" Willy wanted, doubtfully, to know.

"It takes a bit of imagination, I admit, Willy. But I've got a hunch that our chaplain is writhing under the restraint of not being allowed to proclaim his true nature. I don't think it would take much to goad him into making it public. If you, Willy, for example, in your capacity as senior master, should sternly warn him that trips into Boston with headmasters' handsome young secretaries will cause talk and must not be repeated, I'll bet he'll explode and spill the beans. A case of open homosexuality in the sanctity of the school chapel in addition to the Castor business should be as good as fecal stains on a bed sheet."

Willy's lips puckered with disgust at the image, but Tim's idea nonetheless struck him. Did it not offer him a visible way of implementing his pledge to the chairman without any risk to his position on the faculty, no matter what the outcome of the assault upon the headmaster? If he was accused of harshness to young Studebaker, the chaplain, could he not explain it as a merely overzealous concern with the school's reputation?

He entered Jim Studebaker's small office in a transept of the chapel the very next day, looking stern and grave, and closing the door behind him. The chaplain jumped from his chair in surprise at the arrival of so important a visitor. He was obviously a serious young man, possessed of blond and almost angelic good looks.

"Why, Mr. Weldon! What can I do for you?"

Willy seated himself in the chair before the chaplain's desk with a slow and stately dignity. "It's not what you can *do*, my friend. It's what you had better stop doing."

And he proceeded in measured tones to specify just what deductions might be drawn from the "surreptitious" visits to Boston of two young men whose strong mutual affection had already attracted some attention on the campus. Studebaker listened without interrupting, at first with an air of gaping incredulity and finally with eyes aflash with indignation.

"People must have a great appetite for scandal at Averhill," he retorted at last, "if they can find it in anything as innocent as a trip to Boston to take in a matinee."

"In such a case, Studebaker, the appearance is as bad as the crime. To a senior master, anyway, whose duty it is to perceive how things, even innocent things, may appear to others."

"A crime, you say? Even if what the scandalmongers believe were true, would it be a crime?"

"I believe it would, under the old statute."

"You mean, something going back to the witches of Salem? But would it be a crime morally? Today?"

"Any right-minded person would think so."

The chaplain at this seemed to throw caution to the winds. "I can't help wondering if some of these right-minded people aren't driven to such hysteria by fearing the same thing in themselves!"

Willy was now excited with his progress. He moved in for the kill. "Are you suggesting that men with a concern for the school's reputation are perverts at heart?"

"That's not a word I use, Mr. Weldon."

"Is there a better one?"

"Do we need one at all? To describe a perfectly natural relationship between two human beings which is nobody's business but their own? Your word for it should go the way of *kike* and *nigger*."

"A man cannot help being a Jew or a black," Willy rebuked him. "But he can certainly help being a homosexual. And he certainly should!"

The chaplain had risen to his feet. His hands were trembling. "That is a subject, sir, on which we must agree to disagree."

Willy also rose and turned to take his leave. "Very well, Studebaker. But I warn you, here and now, that if you are tempted to air any of your views on this detestable subject to any student on this campus or cause further scandal in the way you spend your free time, your retention of your present post will be brief."

Willy was elated at how easy it had been to bring the young man to the very edge of revolt. Time, and not much of that, could be counted on to finish the job. He telephoned Spencer and related the incident jubilantly.

"Good work, Weldon!" was the gruff response. "When this thing breaks, I'll see to it that the press interviews the chaplain. Who else more proper than the guardian of the school soul? And I'll give you ten to one that he spills his guts on the love that dares not call its name!"

Two days later Willy had another opportunity to strike a blow in the chairman's battle without the least danger to himself. A new and powerful member of the school trustees, the multimillion-dollar heiress Mrs. Myron Fox, a devout Roman Catholic who had nonetheless chosen to send her son to a largely Protestant school for reasons of social advantage, wished to tour the institution over whose destinies she had elected to preside, and no one less than the senior master had been appointed to be her guide.

Taking her on a visit to the infirmary, Willy had decided

to enter it through the dispensary rather than the main hall, and he had deliberately chosen to pause, presumably to speak to a nurse, before a table exhibiting a tray whose contents Mrs. Fox could not help noticing. They were condoms.

"Mr. Weldon!" the lady exclaimed. "Are these things what I think they are?"

He followed her glance and affected a shudder. "I'm afraid so, ma'am."

"If they're for the men who work on the place, the janitors and so forth, I suppose it's none of my business, but why on earth are they put out here, where the students—even the girls—may see them?"

"But, Mrs. Fox, they are *for* the students!"

"Good God in heaven, Mr. Weldon, what are you telling me? Does the headmaster know of this?"

"The headmaster ordered it. He says we must keep up with the times."

Mrs. Fox had no response. She followed him into the infirmary and finished her inspection of the school grounds. Her continued silence was sinister.

The filing of the two suits against the school occurred in the next week, and the press coverage was astonishingly broad. Astonishing, that is, to those who did not know how hard Donald Spencer had been at work. His greatest coup was to induce the nationally known Paula Preston to interview Rosina Castor on her popular television news commentary.

"Our subject tonight involves the socially impeccable and

highly exclusive New England preparatory school Averhill.
If you had thought that those privileged little boys and girls,
overfed, overhoused, and overclothed, as one wit has put it,
were scrupulously minding their p's and q's, we have Rosina
Castor with us tonight to convey a different impression. It
is the burden of her suit against the school that her son was
subjected to violent sexual abuse."

The school chaplain, interviewed by a Boston paper, did
not help to allay the public indignation by maintaining that
if there was any truth in the allegations of the suits, which he
didn't admit, any misconduct had been caused by society's
unreasonable prejudice against certain sexual acts, the arbi-
trary prohibition of which could lead to violence.

As the flames of the scandal raged over the landscape of
the preparatory schools, the wiser headmasters murmured,
"There, but for the grace of God, go I," but the consensus of
opinion was that Averhill was in a bad way indeed, and that
its administration had to be in some way at fault. Donald
Spencer, together with three trustees including Mrs. Fox,
took it upon themselves, without waiting for a formal meeting of the board, to issue a statement to the press that they
were deeply concerned about the moral questions presented
by the lawsuits to the administration of the school.

9

ERWIN C. CALDWELL puffed slowly away at his cigar as he sat in the comfortable back seat of his Silver Cloud Rolls-Royce limousine as it glided through the lovely Massachusetts countryside on its way to Averhill School. He was a large man; stout, strong, bald-headed, and more formidable in appearance than there was any need for him, or really any great desire in him, to be. He had already got pretty much everything out of the world that he had wanted, and having contented himself, he had no particular desire to impress anyone else, including his son, Edward (Bossy), seated silently in the jump seat ahead of him. It was a comfortable enough seat, with a soft back and arm rests, though still a jump seat, but the boy would no more have pointed out that there was room for him beside his parent in the back than would his mild, semi-invalid mother have complained of being always left at home. It was hard to call Erwin Caldwell a tyrant because his rule was never questioned.

He had sent his only son to Averhill not because he had the slightest admiration of, or desire to mingle with, an eastern seaboard upper class very different from the humbler one of his own origin, but because he thought that the Averhill stamp might give the boy a slight advantage in the Wall Street financial world to which he was destined. Erwin's aim in his own life had been to play every card that he was dealt, or that he could arrange to be dealt, to its greatest advantage, with a total disregard to any moral or even cultural association with the card played or with the nature of the play. Viewing his son objectively—as he did everything else—he could not see that the school had made much of a dent in the boy, but he was perfectly willing to concede that this might not be the fault of the institution and that Edward might be poor material to work on. If that were so, it was not something to get overwrought about. It was simply another problem to be faced.

His own fortune had been acquired in lumber from the Brazilian rain forest with a ruthless disregard, that he never stooped to defend, for all ecological or even legal restraints. Unlike many tycoons he had no interest in cloaking his piratical methods in the robes of industrial creativity, nor did he in any way deplore the efforts of liberal-minded statesmen to oppose the headlong destruction of our environment. He was a man of equable temper; he rarely found anything worth getting angry about. That he should take and others resist his taking seemed to him simply the way of the world.

And so with this business at Averhill. Erwin had listened patiently to his son's account of what had happened in his dormitory that night and had not supposed that he was getting an unprejudiced version. He had never known the boy as a disciple of truth; he had too often observed him to mitigate the rigor of that rule. He had sent for Edward to come home and explain the affair; now he was accompanying him back to school for the purpose of having a frank talk with the headmaster. He looked at his watch. Sayre was to receive him at three. They would be just on time.

He broke his silence as they approached the school grounds. "How long will it take you, Edward, to get ready, if I decide, after talking to Mr. Sayre, to take you home with me?"

"You're thinking of taking me out of school, sir?"

"Just answer the question, please."

"I suppose I could pack up in an hour."

"Then do so while I'm having my interview with Mr. Sayre. I may or may not decide to take you home after I've seen him, but I want you to be ready in any case. Be sure to take enough clothes for a possibly long stay."

"But what will I tell my dorm master, sir?"

"Tell him to put any questions he has to the headmaster."

"And may I ask *you* a question, sir?"

"Go ahead."

"If you take me out of school, will it be for good?"

"It will be for *your* good. But I haven't made up my mind about that yet. It all depends on what I learn from the headmaster. It may be that you will stay at school and graduate. It may be that you'll go to Brazil. You'll just have to trust me, that's all."

"Oh, I'll always trust you, sir, of course! But I'd love to go back to Brazil!"

"Unfortunately, in a case like this, your inclinations cannot be consulted."

The big car rolled through the open grilled gates of the Averhill campus and pulled up beside the headmaster's door.

"Tell Patrick to take you to your dormitory and bring you back here when you're packed," Erwin directed his son as he descended from the vehicle. "Wait for me in the car and don't talk to anyone."

A maid ushered Erwin into the headmaster's study where he found Michael waiting for him.

"I'm very quick about my business, sir, and I won't take up much of your valuable time," Erwin began as he took his seat before the central desk. "I appreciate your seeing me on such short notice."

"Of course, Mr. Caldwell, I am deeply sympathetic about your trouble. I can only tell you that we are doing our best to work out some kind of settlement of these suits so that your boy will not be dragged into a sordid court trial."

"That, of course, is to be avoided at all costs. But I should tell you at once, Mr. Sayre, that my lawyers have fully briefed me on all aspects of the legal situation, and I have not come to discuss these at all. I have come for one purpose only, and that is to hear your exact account of what each boy told you after they were apprehended in the dormitory that night."

132 · LOUIS AUCHINCLOSS

"I shall be glad to do that, Mr. Caldwell. And I'm happy to assure you that my memory is a fairly sharp one." Michael proceeded to relate, carefully and precisely, his talk with each boy while Erwin intently listened, never once interrupting. But when Michael had finished he was ready with this comment:

"Castor at first maintained that my son had used force? His initial claim, in short, was that he had been raped?"

"He didn't use that term."

"But that was it, was it not?"

"Yes, but he retracted it."

"And you determined that his retraction absolved you of any duty to report the incident to the Massachusetts authorities?"

"Just so. There was nothing that had to be reported. In my opinion, anyway."

"In your opinion, Mr. Sayre, exactly. And it's your opinion that I'm trying to get at. If you had really believed my son's story that he had been subjected to a malicious and damaging assault on his character, why did you sit by impassively when these suits were filed? Why didn't you use your lawyers, your public relations counsel, your anything and everything, to shout to the world that a dastardly lie had been told about an innocent boy in your school?"

"Mr. Caldwell!" Michael was clearly startled by the sudden strength of his visitor's language. "What had gone on in that cubicle may not have been rape, but it was not exactly what many people call innocent. I did not conceive it my duty to prejudge the case one way or another and add more mud to that already flung."

"Or did you simply suspect that neither boy had told you the whole story?"

"You forget, sir, that these things are never all black or white. Different emotions and reactions get involved in an affair like this."

"In other words, you *do* have some doubt as to whether my boy used force! At least in the beginning. That is what I'm getting at. That is what may explain your impassive attitude in this whole matter. You have no sympathy for either side. Which can only mean that there's something you haven't told me."

"Mr. Caldwell, I don't see what you're driving at. Surely you can't want me to convince you that your son was a rapist!"

"I want to know what you really think! I suspect you have a shrewd idea of what actually happened that night, and I want the truth! Once I have the truth, I can decide how I'm going to handle it. That's how I've always managed my life, and I'm not going to change it now, no matter what the cost or to whom. So please do me the honor of being utterly frank. Was there anything at all that caused you in retrospect to doubt if my son had told you the whole truth and nothing but the truth?"

Michael looked down at his blotter for a moment, and then stroked his forehead. He seemed deeply agitated. "There was one thing," he breathed at last. "Something my wife noted when I told her about it."

"Ah!"

"Your son told me that when Castor came into his cubicle to tell him he couldn't sleep he had complained that he was worried over his mother having a cancer scare. It was true that his mother had had one a month or so before and had sent for him to be with her, but she had been given a clean bill of health, and the boy had returned to school. Your son knew of the incident, as he had had to check Castor out of the dorm at the time, and it occurred to me, or rather to my wife, that if your son had wanted to create a picture of how a worried boy had won his sympathy that night, it might help to show him as worrying about his mother, and that incident might have sprung to mind."

"But did the Castor boy say anything about a cancer scare to my son?"

"Well, of course, we don't know. But my wife, playing backgammon with the boy on a parlor night after I had closed the case and before Castor had been taken home, had inquired, with a hostess's benignity, if his mother had had any further alarms, and he had said no. He had even seemed surprised that she should have asked. So it seems unlikely that he would have complained about that to your son."

"I see, Mr. Sayre. And that is all I need. I am grateful for your time." Erwin rose to depart.

Michael seemed much surprised. "But surely there is more for us to discuss than just that!"

"No. I'm quite satisfied, thank you."

An hour later Erwin and his son were speeding through the twilight in a direction that suddenly startled Bossy.

"Daddy, do you suppose Patrick knows where he's going? We're on the turnpike headed for Boston."

"Patrick knows exactly where he's going. He's headed for the airport where our company jet awaits us for a night flight to Rio. Don't worry. I have your passport and everything."

"Oh, boy, what a lark! Will we go to the Amazon?"

"You may be going to quite a few places, my boy. But you must always remember to do exactly what I tell you."

☙ 10 ☙

THE UNEXPLAINED DISAPPEARANCE of Bossy Caldwell erupted like a clap of thunder in the heavy air over Averhill and reached far enough south seemingly to threaten the very glass in the windows of Donald Spencer's Wall Street office. He had immediately summoned an emergency meeting of the executive committee of the school's board of trustees, a majority of whom were New Yorkers, and some six of whom managed to be solemnly present on an early morning in March. The first hour of the meeting had been devoted to a careful review of all the facts involved.

"I have finally been able to get in touch with Erwin Caldwell," Donald announced to the attentive group. "As you all know he is in charge of a vast lumbering operation in Brazil where he has presumably taken his son. He is back in his office here now, but he has flatly refused to discuss with me his reasons for withdrawing the boy from school. He informed me bluntly that a parental decision prompted by a concern over the boy's health was nobody's business but his own, and he instructed me to see that any property his son had left with any bills owing should be forwarded to him. Not another word could be got out of him, and knowing the man as I do, I can assure you that none will."

"But what can the man be after?" the large, loud, volatile Mrs. Fox demanded. "Surely he must see that hiding away a youth who has been accused of virtual rape before the case has even come to trial is a virtual admission of guilt?"

"Maybe he sees his son's case as a hopeless one," suggested Leonard Chase, a prominent Wall Street lawyer, a man of noted suavity and charm, famed for his skillful handling of baffled juries in complicated corporate litigations. "And by removing his son altogether from the reach of a court he may think he can hamstring the Castors' ability to prove their case. It's a kind of desperate remedy but he may deem the situation a desperate one."

"But can't the boy be brought back if necessary?" Mrs. Fox inquired. "Can't he be—what's the term?—extradited?"

"Can you extradite a witness? Don't forget the Caldwell boy is not a defendant in either of the two cases. The school is."

"And regardless of what the law is," Donald concluded, "I think we can all agree that Erwin Caldwell has not only the will but the ability to hide his son in the jungles of Brazil in such a way that the president of the United States and the entire Marine Corps could never get their hands on him. And anyway I doubt that the Castors are even particularly interested in nabbing Bossy Caldwell. I think they regard him as a mere factor of the evil emanating from the headmaster's policies. It's the school—the school remodeled by Michael Sayre—that is the subject of their ire. I suspect that Mrs. Castor believes that what happened to her boy is a common occurrence on our campus and that she is using a moral hose to clean the place out!" Donald cast a shrewd glance around the long table at which they were assembled and shrugged. "Who knows? Maybe the woman has a point."

"*Quelle horreur!*" exclaimed Mrs. Fox in unexpected French.

"In any case," lawyer Chase opined, "there can be no doubt that the flight of young Caldwell has contributed to the danger of these two suits. The school is unquestionably more vulnerable."

"And not only to big damages assessed by a jury probably already prejudiced against private schools for what they believe are millionaires' children," Donald stressed, "but also to a sad loss of reputation in the public at large. And then, of course, there's the horrid question of what this may do to our forthcoming fund drive."

"Our refusal even to consider a settlement has to be rethought," the lawyer agreed.

"Is it really as bad as all that?" Myra Pickens, youngest of the trustees but far from the least active, was the bright, pert, black-eyed partner in a successful hedge fund, with a young son at the school and a mind as liberal as the headmaster's. She was known to enjoy needling the older members of the board with sharp reminders that their views were dated. "Don't you think enough of us are on to the fact that Mrs. Castor may be the kind of vindictive old bitch who goes bonkers every time her little boy thinks another boy has so much as touched him?"

"I see no reason for using such strong language about the mother of one of our students," Mrs. Fox retorted with considerable hauteur. "The poor woman's son may well have been the subject of a nefarious assault. You should have more respect, Mrs. Pickens, for her feelings and what she has been put through."

"I'm sorry, Mrs. Fox. I didn't realize I was speaking of one of your pals."

This did little to appease her opponent. "Mrs. Castor doesn't happen to be what you call one of my pals. We are not even acquainted. But I still feel for her pain—even her agony—under the circumstances. And I also feel that we on the board must face up to our responsibility for the conditions in the school that have led up to the tragic incident."

"Isn't 'tragic' putting it rather strongly? Can any of us be so naive as not to be aware of the kind of thing that goes on between young males with rapidly developing sexual drives when they find themselves alone together? You can't watch them every minute of the day and night!"

"They can be controlled, Mrs. Pickens! They can have drilled into them what is right and what is very, very wrong! That is a school's job, Mrs. Pickens! Would you turn it into a brothel?"

Donald saw that it was time to intervene. "Mrs. Fox has a point. We can't just stick our heads in the sand like a bunch of ostriches. We have to face the facts of juvenile sexuality and just how we're going to handle it. We also have to assess how it has *been* handled. Even how it has been handled by those we very much admire. I don't think I have to tell any of you here how deeply I like and respect Michael Sayre. As all of you know, we were classmates at school here and have worked together ever since for the betterment of our beloved institution. Inevitably, we have not always agreed. You're all aware, I'm sure, that recently Michael and I have not quite seen eye to eye on the question of expanding our sporting facilities—"

"I'd call it something more than not quite seeing eye to eye," Leonard Chase interrupted with a dry laugh. "It sounded to me more like the opening guns of World War Three."

"Our learned counsel always has to have his little joke," Donald replied mildly enough, though he had to swallow to repress his snarl. "But there was nothing in our differences that couldn't be straightened out with a little more talk. Now we are faced with a much deeper crisis. Michael, with the best of intentions, I do not doubt, in a sincere desire to spare the school the odium of a sexual scandal, has done his best to make what I fear was a criminal assault on the innocence of a minor appear in the light of a far less pernicious though still wrongful species of adolescent sexual experimentation."

"Still very wrongful," grumbled Mrs. Fox.

"Oh, don't misunderstand me, Corbina. Of course it is. I'm simply distinguishing between a crime and a misdemeanor. The latter is something all schools face. It is an unfortunate aspect of the academic picture. Rape is not. Rape can destroy a school."

"You're going pretty far there, Donald," the lawyer objected. "Anything like rape in our case is a long way from being proved."

"It's less of a long way since Erwin Caldwell flew his son to Brazil," Donald insisted. "What I keep getting back to is what we must do to bolster Averhill's tottering reputation. We have to give the academic community some reasonable reassurance not only that we deeply regret what has occurred, but that it can never happen again!"

"By which, I take it, you mean we should toss someone's head to the angry mob?" The lawyer's tone was now frankly hostile.

Donald needed more time, but he decided he couldn't wait. He had to meet the challenge. "You might put it that way, yes."

"And considering that this meeting has been called an executive session, with the express purpose of not inviting the headmaster, I assume that the head under consideration is his?"

"Whose else, sir? Whose else could we offer? Michael has received full credit for all the good things that have happened to Averhill in the three years of his administration. He is also answerable for the bad. I am not now asking you to vote his deposition. I am telling you that it is one of our possibilities. If we decide that Michael deliberately covered up a crime on the campus and failed in his duty to report a complaint of it to the state authorities, I cannot see why this board would be acting either harshly or unreasonably in seeking his resignation. Duty is duty. The fact that it is painful for us, and particularly painful for one who was such a friend as I—"

"I think, Donald, that we've heard enough about that famous friendship," snapped Chase, in a now overt declaration of war. "This whole wretched matter has given you as much pain, I'm sure, as it gave you and Corbina Fox to give your speculations to the press without consulting the board!"

"Why, Mr. Chase, how dare you imply—" Mrs. Fox was demanding when Donald raised his voice.

"Please, please, both of you! I will say no more about friendship. This matter is too serious to be lost in personal recriminations. I think under the circumstances we had better adjourn and think things over in solitude. I have stated my case. I simply ask you each and all to come back to me with your ideas on the subject."

"I can give you mine here and now!" Chase announced as he rose. "I consider the headmaster's discussions with the two boys involved, and his decision on how to act or not act in the case, as matters totally within his discretion and into which I do not choose to inquire. The Castors and the state authorities are acting, of course, as they see fit, and it is equally our prerogative to challenge in court their standing to interfere with our disciplinary measures. If a reasonable settlement will buy them off, it should be considered, but I would be reluctant to offer them Michael Sayre's scalp."

Donald, alone in the room after the meeting had noisily and even protestingly adjourned, decided that it was probably just as well that he had learned what he would be up against in ousting Michael from his job. Leonard Chase was a formidable opponent and would almost certainly gather enough votes on the board to check even a reprimand of the headmaster. The only feasible way to get rid of Michael was somehow to induce him to get rid of himself.

Donald telephoned now to Elias Castor, whom he had known as a fellow student at Averhill and later as a fellow parent. He had correctly divined that he would more easily touch base with the husband than with the wife, knowing Elias as a man who would probably regard the whole matter of his son and the Caldwell boy as a source for his own amusement. He could be counted on, therefore, to persuade his impassioned spouse to attend a conference with the chairman of the school board that she otherwise might turn down flat. Elias wanted a front seat at the play, and Donald soon received a bid to be present at the Castors' house that same day at five o'clock. He found Mrs. Castor in a gilded salon, the silent and grim occupant of a large Louis XVI bergère on whose back rested the hands of her standing husband, smirking with the air of a court jester awaiting his chance for a clever crack.

"Mrs. Castor," Donald began gravely, "I wish to start by offering you my heartfelt sympathy for the terrible experience to which you and your son have been subjected." He had the instinct to feel that the omission of her husband would not damage his case.

"You surprise me, sir," was the equally grave retort from the bergère. "Counsel for the institution of which you are chairman have rejected my petition in toto. Nor has a single word of sympathy or regret come to me from any official of the school."

"Surely you must be aware, Madam, that the moment a litigation is even threatened, a defendant's lips are sealed by counsel. The silence to which you refer does not mean in the least that the hearts of many of the Averhill community do not bleed for you. *I* can certainly state that in my own case I harbor a state of outrage at the treatment accorded you."

"Are you telling me, Mr. Spencer, that you had no power to alter the situation?"

"I am telling you, Mrs. Castor, that had I attempted to do so, I should have been overridden by my board. They were following the old rule that when a wrong is charged, one's first step must be a sweeping denial of any involvement at all. The way is thus cleared for a complete trial of the facts. And may I suggest, Mrs. Castor, that your own counsel would have given us the same advice had we retained them. That is the American lawyer. I'm not saying he's right."

Mrs. Castor seemed slightly mollified by this. She turned around to her husband who nodded as if to approve Spencer's thought. She turned back to her guest. "I'm not that enchanted with the American lawyer myself, Mr. Spencer. But I guess we're stuck with him."

"Not entirely, Ma'am. We can still talk to each other, as you and I are doing now. And perhaps we can even make some progress. Without a stiff fee, too. I see no reason why two persons as clear-headed as you and I cannot, in a frank and private interchange involving none but ourselves and committing us to nothing, seek the truth in the problem spread before us. Do I have your confidence, Ma'am?"

"Proceed, Mr. Spencer."

"I suggest then that we start with a consideration of the school under Mr. Sayre's leadership and what this has led to. His purpose, as he frankly stated, was to bring a belated institution into a modern world. That sounds well enough, and it might have been had he limited himself to the good things in the modern world. But Mr. Sayre seemed to want all of it, the bitter as well as the sweet. Young people were to be free to express themselves in coarse language and sexual license, unfettered by the restraints of old-fashioned manners or the limiting standards of good taste. If someone went too far, like the Caldwell boy forcing his unwanted attentions on a younger student, well, that was simply a matter, was it not, for a behavioral therapist. Such things were not so much moral problems as growing pains and should be handled accordingly. There was no need, was there, for people to get excited about it?"

"Goodness gracious, Mr. Spencer," Mrs. Castor cried out, "you make me think the school is as bad as Venusberg in *Tannhäuser*!"

"A good analogy for old opera fans like you and me. And it's sad to think that all this was the work of one sincere but misguided man. If he can only be gently but firmly removed from his post, I have little doubt that the school could be returned to its normal and once reputable course. And you, my dear lady, may have the golden opportunity to help us bring this about."

"Me? What are you talking about, Mr. Spencer? How?"

"If you and I can agree to settle your case in the way I am about to outline, I believe I could induce Mr. Sayre to resign. Wouldn't that, plus an apology to your son, satisfy you? Your concern is not, I deduce, with the beastly Caldwell boy. He is just a bug that the headmaster's policies have let loose in the school. Nor can I really believe that you are interested in monetary damages. You want a wrong righted, isn't that it?"

"It's true that money was never a first consideration with me," Mrs. Castro said doubtfully. "It was my lawyer's suggestion."

"Of course! And he'd have got half of it, wouldn't he?"

"Something like that, I suppose."

"You can be sure of it. You and I are not here to enrich the bar, Mrs. Castor. We have higher motives. More public-spirited ones. My proposal of an apology plus the resignation of the man whose misguided rule has caused all this misery to you and yours should be enough to satisfy your injured honor without subjecting your boy to the trauma of having to relate his shame in a courtroom and be subject to the humiliating cross-examination of opposing counsel, trying to trap him in a lie."

"Oh, Mr. Spencer, you're right! You're right!"

"I had the feeling, from the wonderful things I have heard

of you, Mrs. Castor, that you and I were people who would soon come to an understanding."

"Oh, we think alike! We do!"

"Maybe I'd better leave the two of you alone," inserted the grinning Elias. "I know when a husband is *de trop.*"

"Oh, Elias, you should have your mouth washed out with soap!" But she was smiling, and when Donald left, an agreement had been made.

11

IT DID LITTLE to brighten the darkness of Michael's mood that the topic for discussion that morning in his sixth-form class was Napoleon, to his thinking the most sinister of all great historical figures.

"It has been estimated," he began in a somber tone, "that only Jesus, in all the millions of pages in world tongues, has been the subject of more written words than Napoleon Bonaparte. And if you adopt the orthodox Christian position that Jesus was God, it leaves the little corporal as the most discussed of mortals."

His long pause after this introduction led one boy to suppose he was awaiting a comment.

"Well, there was never a greater conqueror, was there, sir? Alexander the Great seems puny in contrast. And Genghis Khan and Attila and Tamerlane were more like plagues than real conquerors, weren't they?"

"Maybe that's what conquerors are," a girl intervened.

"But Wellington defeated him," another girl pointed out. "Doesn't that make Wellington the greater man?"

"It took the whole of Europe to defeat him, really," Michael observed. "That and a Russian winter. Some historians think he was at his greatest in defeat. His accomplishments were, of course, phenomenal. At one point or another his armies stood in every European capital from Moscow to Madrid. It seemed at times that nothing could stop him. He owned so much of the world that he had to sell some of it off, which was how we got the Louisiana territory, one-third of our nation. Even some philosophers who maintain that history is made up of the flux and reflux of masses rather than by the ambitions and acts of individuals are apt to admit that Napoleon was the one figure who made his own dent in it. As Henry Adams put it, no one knew what Napoleon would do, but everyone knew that what he did would determine the matter."

"He wasn't a greater general than Lee, was he, sir?" This inquiry came from one of the school's few southern boys.

"That is certainly debatable, Harry," Michael replied. "But I don't want to get into the analysis of battles. I'm sure that you're better at it than I am. Today I want to get into what all the gunpowder and glory amounts to. Did Lee's unquestionable military genius accomplish anything but the prolongation of the misery of the South?"

"It gave us our finest hour, sir," was the stout reply.

"Did that bring back the three hundred thousand boys you lost?"

"No, but it helped."

"That's a good answer, Harry. If it is an answer."

One of Michael's star pupils, an eager, pushing youth from Philadelphia, now took up the cause of the French emperor. "It wasn't just conquest, sir! Napoleon was resisting the old despots of Europe. He represented the enlightenment of the French Revolution! Not the terror, of course, but the spirit of liberty."

"But, Tony, he suppressed liberty of speech. He muzzled the press. He restored the old aristocracy. He even invited the pope to crown him!"

Tony muttered something about omelet and eggs, and the room tittered, not loudly, for Michael commanded respect.

"And what about the Code Napoléon?" someone in the back row asked. "Wasn't that supposed to be a good thing?"

"People are always pointing that out," Michael conceded. "But I never know quite what they mean by it. It's not so hard to write a good law. The Abbé Sieyès wrote many constitutions in that day, some of them perhaps quite good. But people wouldn't live by them." He turned now to his main theme. "Why do we reserve our greatest admiration for mighty warriors even when their victories bring disaster upon us? For twenty years Napoleon took his people from glory to glory. He had countless opportunities to pause and make peace and savor his victories, but he always insisted on pushing on. In the end, after France had lost a generation of her finest men, she found herself reduced to the same borders she had had at the beginning. And for this she worshipped and still worships Napoleon beyond any other man in her history! Is it for this that she is considered the most cultivated of nations? Is glory everything? Will glory save us from the atom?"

But the class disappointed him. They seemed reluctant to pursue a train of thought so abstract. The hour soon exhausted itself in a heated debate of whether or not Napoleon should have kept the Louisiana territory. Some claimed it was too large and remote to be defended against inevitable American encroachment. Others pointed out that the man who could dispatch a million men to the steppes of Russia could have sent a few thousand to our Midwest, which would have been an ample force against an almost unarmed America. Besides, it was darkly suggested, the Indians always joined the French.

Michael, who would ordinarily have had no difficulty in focusing the class on the larger topic of war and peace, was too preoccupied that day to do much more than idly listen to the chatter. His mind kept running back and forth over the lines of the secret memorandum that Donald Spencer had sent up to him from New York by a special messenger. It contained his account of the Castors' willingness to drop their suit on certain conditions and his assurance that Massachusetts would certainly drop its suit if this were obtained. The memorandum ended as follows:

> I urge you, my old friend, which you are despite all our differences, to give this your deepest consideration. The flight of the Caldwell boy seems to have almost assured a proof of the charge of rape, and your action, or failure to

act under the circumstances, will be proclaimed by our enemy to be a near criminal cover-up. The withdrawal of the claim for damages is, of course, an advantage for the school, but the great thing would be the saving of our reputation. You have already accomplished many of the things you wished to accomplish in your tenure, and nobody need know the reason for your resignation. The Castors have agreed to silence on all matters but the apology, and everyone knows, in our era of cripplingly expensive litigation, that a settlement premised on an apology is no real admission of guilt. You will have a world of other offers. Do this for Averhill!

Michael was not for a moment taken in by these weasel words. He knew what Donald was after and could even admire the skill with which he went about obtaining it. Donald knew that he would lose if he called on the board to do his dirty work for him. This way he was handing Michael the noose and inviting him to stick his neck in it. It was clever, for Michael was strongly tempted to do so. He was utterly disgusted at how much was being made of what two boys might or might not have done in bed at night and of how preoccupied a great school could be with the randy couplings of juvenile males. He wanted to get out, to breathe fresh air, to shout at the parents and trustees to take their bloody academy and . . . ! The prospect of a public trial was even more nauseating, with prying, insinuating, grinning counsel perhaps implying that the headmaster was himself some sort of perverted voyeur who smacked his lips at a vision of buggery!

And then, too, quite aside from the avoidance of sordid exposures, Spencer's little plot would save the school the cost of damages and the interference of the state. And Spencer was quite right that nobody would take seriously an apology rendered, so to speak, at gun point. Averhill *would* be saved a staining experience. And as to himself, would a resignation really cost him much? Retirement after only a brief term had become common enough among private school heads in an era where once fundamental principles of administration were under constant reexamination. It was no disgrace for a headmaster to find himself in disaccord with his board or his parents or his faculty. There would be some gossip and speculation, of course, but the whole matter would soon be as dead as her late majesty Queen Anne, and there would be plenty of opportunities for one of Michael's good record. What about that foundation of which Ione had spoken? And where Ione was concerned, hadn't he agonized over her failure to find a satisfactory role for herself at Averhill? What was he waiting for?

That very evening, over their usual nightcap, he put this question to his wife. "Do you think the Gladwin Foundation might still be interested if I agreed to go down for an interview?"

Ione was already in her nightgown and sitting up in bed, a drink in one hand, the other idly turning the pages of a fashion magazine. He was standing before her tying the belt of his robe. She looked up quickly and then put her glass on the bedside table with a sharp click. "What the devil do you mean by *that?*"

"Simply that it might not be the wisest thing in the world for me to turn my back on even such a crack of an opening as you suggested."

"Michael, come off it! What's happened?"

"This has happened, darling."

He turned to remove the Spencer memorandum from his coat pocket and handed it to her. She seized it and read it intently without a motion or a word. Then she looked up at the ceiling for a moment of thought before rereading the document. He simply watched her.

"I never read such garbage," she said at last. "Will you even answer it?"

"Darling, I'm thinking very seriously of acting on it. It's not at all a bad settlement for the school. My real job here is more than half done, and a great foundation is a great opportunity. For both of us."

"Not at this price—never." She tore the memorandum in two and threw the pieces on the floor. "Have you gone crazy, my dearest? Do you think Gladwin would so much as look at you if you came to them with a stain like that?"

"Why would Gladwin even know?"

"Because they go over every candidate with a microscope! And even if they missed it, do you think *I* would ever allow you to accept such a stain?"

"Ione, my sweet, it's not that bad. And, anyway, Gladwin or no Gladwin, you and I could have our wonderful old life back again. You know you haven't been exactly in love with

Averhill. Oh, you've been good as gold about it, I know, but it's never really been your cup of tea, and—"

"Well, from now on it's going to be!" she broke in passionately. She got out of bed now to throw her arms around his neck. "Darling, give me another chance! Please, please, please! I want to show you what I can do. We're going to fight this thing till the wretched Spencer will wish he'd never been born!"

"Ione! Will you listen to reason?"

"No! And if you so much as threaten again to quit your job here, do you know what I'll do?"

"What?"

"I'll answer that from the hotel in Reno where I'll be establishing my residence for a divorce."

Michael laughed as he kissed her. "I guess that does it," he conceded.

12

IN THE AFTERMATH of their joint resolution to fight the Castors to the death and when the exuberance of their accord had died down a bit, Ione was obliged to realize that she had really no armies to throw into the field. It was all very well to assume that Michael would defeat Spencer in any overt attempt to oust him, but could she be sure of that? A proven case that he had condoned a rape might create such a division in the board that Michael might feel compelled to quit for the good of the school!

She could only leave the house and stroll to the river, despite the constant rain, to mull things over, her eyes now sometimes smarting with hot tears. For if she had just let Michael alone when he was inclined to give in on the sports arena question, Spencer would have been his stoutest ally in this Castor matter. Together they would have annihilated the silly suits. But because she had hoped that an uncompromising resistance to the sports issue would result in his dignified and understandable resignation as headmaster and begin a better life for both of them, she had talked him into taking a position that was now resulting in possible ruin.

If she had acted solely for his good, she could have forgiven herself. But she was too honest not to face the fact that she had acted because she was bored at school, that she had been willing to risk her husband's career for her own satisfaction. It was unbearable.

She decided the next day to go to New York and find out what her mother thought about the whole situation. She told her husband that she had to see her old dentist and took the train to Grand Central. Diane met her for lunch at Lutece, her favorite French restaurant. Of course, she knew all about her son-in-law's trouble, and she listened quietly to Ione's rehash, but on the main question she was wholly negative.

"The foundation would never touch Michael if he's expelled," she said sadly. "Of course, in time these things are forgotten or glossed over, but by then the position will have been filled."

"I feel so helpless," Ione complained. "Can you, Mother, who've survived so many office rumbles, imagine any way I can do something for poor Michael?"

"There's not much a headmaster's wife can do, is there? You can talk to trustees, yes, but it's so obvious to them that you have to say what you're saying. All they can do is sympathize. They're not going to vote for Michael because they're sorry for you. And the faculty won't really have much of a voice in this. Some might have, but you say the older ones may be against Michael anyway. And I doubt you could swing the wretched Spencer around even if you offered to sleep with him. Ugh!" Diane made a face as she recalled Donald's features. "Oh, but that reminds me of something!" She suddenly smiled. "I'm rather surprised actually, now I think of it, that you haven't mentioned it yourself."

"I suppose you're thinking of Elias Castor."

"Damn right I'm thinking of Elias Castor. You knew him, of course, before either of you were married."

"I did. Not that I remember it with much pleasure."

"Didn't you have an affair with him?"

"Mother! How the hell did you know that?"

"Mothers who keep their eyes open learn more than you think."

"But it was so brief! Actually only one night! And I think I must have been half drunk, or something like that. Do you know, it was the only affair I ever had?"

"I didn't know that. But it hardly surprises me. You were always so serious. You didn't get *that* from your old ma."

"Elias and I couldn't have been more different! I don't think I ever even really liked him."

"One doesn't always have to. The point is not how you felt about him but how he felt about you."

"I don't know!"

"Well, find out."

"Are you suggesting that I should sleep with *him* now?"

"Don't be ridiculous. Your motive would be too apparent. But call him up—if you can do so without his wife's knowing. At his club, maybe. I'm sure he has one, probably several, to get away from her. Ask him to meet you for a drink."

"And do you imagine he'll come?"

"Oh, he'll come all right. He's a cat for curiosity. Remember he worked for me once. Briefly."

"And what shall I say to him?"

"Darling, you have to do something on your own. I can't do it all for you."

It had indeed been a curious affair.

Ione had met Elias Castor shortly after her graduation from law school, at a time when she was feeling discouraged and depressed. Although her grades had been good, she had failed the procedural half of the New York State bar exams, and she had been unsuccessful in her application for a clerkship in the big Wall Street law firm that she had particularly wished to join. She knew, of course, that a failure to pass both halves of the bar on a first try was too common to be much upset about and that there were plenty of other good firms that were apt to be more receptive to her bid, but with the natural exaggeration of youth she had allowed herself to be plunged in gloom and to wonder if she had not chosen the wrong profession.

It was with the design of cheering her up that Diane Fletcher, at one of her and Ira's dinner parties, had seated their daughter next to Elias Castor. It was not that she had any particular admiration for this ebullient young man, but he was lively and amusing and a bit of a buffoon. She had met him at parties in Gotham; despite his youth and idleness and lack of apparent importance, he seemed to go everywhere, one of the briefly taken-up pets of a glittering world. He had even offered one of the little pieces he sometimes wrote on Manhattan social doings to *Style*, and Diane had actually published it. What he lived on nobody knew; he presumably enjoyed some minimal allowance from his highly respectable family, who were reputed to disapprove strongly of his epicurean existence. Diane never dreamed that he would become anything like a beau of Ione's; she had merely hoped that he would get her to laugh.

Which he did.

"Your ma tells me you've had the good sense to bust the silly bars," he began. "My congratulations!"

Ione stared at the funny man. "Why is it a subject for those?"

"Well, won't it relieve you from a life of getting people out of their bargains by crawling through the small print? Even Portia, after cheating poor Shylock out of his bond, had the sense to give it up and go back to her palace and the strapping husband her money had bought."

"But I'm not giving up the law!" Ione protested in surprise. "I'll take the exam again in the spring, and with any luck I should pass."

"Why do all you pretty and charming girls want to be lawyers and dentists and undertakers?" he protested. "Aren't you afraid of becoming as dull as the men? For it's not our sex, you know, that makes us bores. It's our jobs."

"You mean that, idle, you'd all be dazzling wits?"

"Well, wittier, anyway. Read the old French novels about a *désoeuvré* society. The men are always delightful."

"Do *you* work?"

"Heaven forbid!"

"And you think that's kept you from being a bore?"

"Ah, touché! I guess I asked for that one. But you'd better keep on talking to me, for I can assure you the man on your other side is a worse one. So let's chat. What I really want to ask you is, is it fair to other girls for you to have so many assets?"

"What do you mean by 'assets'?"

"Well, to begin with you have the two that are most needed in the game of husband catching: money and beauty. And you only need one for that game. You're playing it with loaded dice."

"Assuming I'm playing it at all," she retorted with some hauteur. "I can't be a judge of my beauty, as you call it, but I can tell you right now that I'm far from being an heiress."

"Yet your parents certainly live well." He gazed admiringly down the well-appointed table.

"I don't know why I'm telling you this, Mr. Castor, but my parents live well because they work hard and earn well. They are not accumulators, either of them. They believe, as I do, in the here and now."

"So you'll be left like Hans Christian Andersen's little match girl to freeze to death in the snow? Dear me, what a pity."

"Don't be ridiculous. They'll look after me. All I'm saying is that I'm not an heiress."

"You mean we can't afford to marry each other?"

"You mean that *you* can't afford to marry me. Well, I must console myself."

"You sound as if that wouldn't be hard. You should have more sympathy for the poor guy who has to marry an heiress."

"Why do you *have* to?"

"How else do you expect me to live, Ione? I may call you that, may I not?" She nodded impatiently. "And the competition is dreadful. All the fellows are after the moneybags. And bags many of them are."

"Are you implying that all heiresses are doomed to be married for their money?"

"Every blessed one of them."

"And never for love?"

"Oh, that may be sometimes thrown in. But it's not essential. In Europe people are more realistic about this—or used to be. The indispensability of the *dot* was frankly recognized. A suitor who withdrew his proposal if the *dot* proved inadequate was deemed a perfectly reasonable young man. But over here we carried our revolution not only against the tyranny of old Europe but against what we saw as its materialism and immorality, blithely ignoring the fact that we ourselves were even more steeped in those qualities. We proclaimed our faith in liberty and love! And our marriages, *all* our marriages had to be based on love, mutual love. The national myth included a picture of the type of man who married for money; he was sly, sleek, mustachioed, foreign, a kind of stage villain. He was held up to our heiresses as a type to avoid, and avoid him they easily did, as he didn't exist. They rarely saw him in his real form: the handsome, broad-shouldered, blond, blue-eyed captain of an Ivy League shell. So accepted was the legend that the groom himself, handing his lacey bride into the Rolls-Royce that would take them from the church to the opulent reception, may not have fully recognized the role played in his courtship by the gleam of his beloved's gold."

Ione at last found herself intrigued. His elocution was so smooth; he might have been reciting a piece he had learned by heart. Perhaps he was. "Heavens! Where does that leave poor girls like me?"

"Oh, you have the other asset. It's more than enough. It might even lure a fortune hunter from his goal."

"Even one as committed as yourself?"

He gave her a sudden strange look. "You know, it might. It really might."

"Even if it meant you had to take a job?"

"Oh, no, no, that might be too much. But wait! Didn't you say you were going to stick to the law? Mightn't you become a partner in one of those great firms? And aren't some of them supposed to make millions?"

"Not many women, I fear."

"But that will change, won't it? Women are advancing everywhere. And I wouldn't have to be entirely useless as a husband. In the evenings you could read your briefs to me. I might even give you some pointers in style. I've written for your ma's magazine, you know."

"But in the evenings you'd be going to your dinner parties, wouldn't you? You couldn't give *them* up. The hostesses of Manhattan, like the Maenads, would tear you in pieces!"

He tapped his forehead. "As Albany says in *Lear:* 'Great thing of us forgot!'"

That, as she began to discover, was the thing about Elias. He read a lot; he loved poetry; he had even once written some. There was a serious side to him if one could only pull it out. He had twice cited Shakespeare in their first colloquy.

The meeting was their introduction to a sometimes acerbic, sometimes hilarious relationship. Elias professed himself at once stricken, as he put it, like a naked Saint Sebastian, a pincushion riddled with the arrows of Eros. He called her constantly to tell her jokes, sometimes off-color ones, accompanied by screams of laughter, and to urge her to go out with him. When she at last agreed to do so, she found that she was diverted. She had started working for Mr. Abrams and was finding the long drudging days in his law library researching obscure points a dismal contrast to the sparkling ones her parents described of their own activities, which she had once tended to look rather down upon. It was something of a relief to dine with the exuberant Elias at a good French restaurant, even when, on a rare occasion, at the end of a meal, he would fling up his hands in mock despair, exhibit an empty pocketbook, and hand her the bill. He somehow made it seem a compliment to her sophistication that they were both above such petty things.

If she was looking for the hidden good in him, he, like a genial satyr, seemed intent on an opposite quest. He never made a pass at her, but he did not hesitate to suggest that an affair with a lover as adroit as Elias Castor might help to make up for the dreary days of the profession to which she had quixotically chosen to enslave herself. He even, and only half-jokingly, maintained that she had carried her natural early resistance to parental rule to puritanical excess and that she had turned herself into a kind of John Knox hurling epithets at the lovely Mary Stuart. Reluctantly amused, she wondered if there might not be some truth in this.

One night at a cabaret he waxed almost serious. She had accused him of being less than truthful on the subject of his own parents, whom he described as tyrants and who she had heard were reputed to be a kindly and sympathetic couple.

"Oh, they didn't beat me, if that's what you mean," he retorted without his usual snicker. "They even loved me, if you like. But they were too greedy for their children's love in return. Why, they always wanted to know, couldn't we be one big happy family? Why? Because the price was too great. My brothers paid it, but I couldn't. I couldn't lie."

"Lie about what?"

"About everything. Oh, it didn't matter if everyone knew it was a lie. It only mattered that you should say it. That you loved Christmas, for example. That you loved Mummy and Daddy more than anything. That you loved baseball, football, and all those horrid sports. That you loved the beach club in summer and the nasty little brats whom you had to play with. That you loved Jesus. That you loved God! You accuse me of untruthfulness, Ione. Well, if there's one thing I stand for in my admittedly rather screwed up existence it's the truth!"

Ione had been impressed by this. It had a good deal to do with what happened that night when, for the first time, she let him come up to her apartment when he took her home. There was also an element of experimentation in it. She had been a virgin longer than many of her friends, and had begun to see the state as an inhibition rather than a virtue. So they copulated. She was always to insist to herself that this was precisely what they had done. They did not become lovers. He professed to be one, but she didn't really believe him, and she herself was certainly not. Nor did they "sleep together," for she sent him home afterward. No, they copulated, purely and simply, and without having previously so much as kissed. He had even chuckled as he pulled down his pants and murmured, "You're going to love this, honey. You really are."

Well, yes, she had liked it. Sort of. But it was never repeated. The next day he appeared unexpectedly at her office and insisted that she go out for lunch with him. When she pleaded that she had to work he threatened to make a scene, and she rapidly consented.

In the restaurant he proposed marriage. He was deadly serious. She tried in vain to make light of it.

"But your heiresses, Eli. What about them?"

"They'll have to do without me, that's all."

"And what do you propose that we should live on?"

"You have a job, and your parents will do something for us. Even mine will if they decide I'm serious and will go to work."

"You could bring yourself to that?"

He smiled and tried to take her hand across the table. But she withdrew it. "You see what you've reduced me to," he reproached her. "You behold passion's slave."

Ione remembered ruefully that her mother had once told her, "Sex is never a thing to play with, my dear. Even I have learned that." For she saw now with a blinding clarity that poor Elias was desperately trying to cast himself in a role he would never be able to sustain. He might have been sincerely in love. He might have truly wished to become a responsible and loving spouse. It might even have been, had she cared to boast about it, which she certainly didn't, a triumph on her part to have subdued so indurated an epicurean to this state, but she could only bitterly regret it. Elias would have to get over this. And, of course, he would get over it.

"The whole thing is quite impossible, Eli," she said gravely now. "I'm not in love with you, and I never could be. You're a good friend, and that's all. And I'm not so fatuous as to imagine that our friendship will survive my refusal to have it become anything more. You will naturally resent me, however unreasonable that may be. Life is like that."

His face showed only too clearly that he had taken in that she really meant it. He made one last try. "Was I that bad last night? I can do better."

"You were fine. That's not it at all."

"What do you suppose this is going to do to me? Have you no sense of responsibility?"

She had to smile. "Of course, it's a blow to your masculine vanity. Men shouldn't take it that way but they do. However, you'll get over that. You can console yourself by thinking what a sad mistake I've made. You may even find yourself a tiny bit relieved."

At last she heard his old laugh. "You're a little devil, Ione! And you're sending me back to the big one!"

Whereupon he abruptly left the table, the restaurant, his unfinished meal, and the bill. Ione gratefully paid it.

Some months later at a Fletcher dinner party Ira informed his daughter that she would be seated by a young man called Michael Sayre.

"He's not another Elias Castor," he observed.

"That may be a point in his favor."

"By the way, what did you ever do with Castor?"

"Nothing."

"Perhaps that's all one can do with him."

🌿 13 🌿

WHEN IONE LOOKED UP in her Social Register the name
of Elias Castor, whom she had not seen, except for a casual
meeting on the street or a glimpse at a social gathering,
for a decade and a half, she was not surprised to find him
listed as a member of no less than four men's clubs. She
telephoned to the first, the Patroons, at five o'clock one
afternoon and was informed that Mr. Castor was indeed
presently in the card room, but could not be disturbed.
She insisted that it was an emergency and boldly gave her
name. Some minutes later she heard Elias's indignant query
in her ear.

"Is that really you, Ione? You should know that we can't
talk except through counsel."

"There's no reason adverse parties to a suit can't meet so
long as both agree to it."

"But I don't agree to it! So please hang up. I want to get
back to my bridge game. The others are waiting for me."

"Eli, I've got to talk to you! For the sake of our old friendship. Please!"

"A fat lot you care about our old friendship! Why should I do anything for you, Ione, after the way you treated me?"

"Because you're a nicer person."

"Oh?" His tone showed some relenting. "But don't you know that if Rosina found out I'd even spoken to you on the phone, she'd take the first plane to Reno?"

"Rosina need never know. Oh, please, Eli!"

"Oh, all right. But give me an hour to finish my bridge game. And then come down here—we'll meet in the bar. No, Rosina's ghastly brother-in-law might be in there, tanking up. I'd better get a private room. Give your name at the door as Mrs. Smith, and I'll leave word you're to be admitted."

An hour later, in a small sitting room hung with hunting prints, Elias silently and somberly consumed two martinis while Ione related the story of the long and bitter conflict between her husband and Donald Spencer and how she had unwittingly contributed to its final and fatal rift.

"And now this terrible case is going to finish off poor Michael," she concluded dolefully. "And it's all my fault!"

Elias shook his head. "I don't agree it's that, and I'm sorry for your trouble. But I cannot fathom what you expect me to do about it or even why you're here at all."

"That's what I'm coming to. Michael is convinced that your son is lying to clear himself and keep the truth from his mother. That would be a perfectly natural thing for a scared boy to do. Throw the blame on another, particularly an older boy, a bully, and a prefect of the school who had no business being in his cubicle. Oh, Eli, if you could only make your son realize the damage he is causing and that telling the truth is really not going to hurt him all that much!"

Elias's eyes gleamed with sudden humor. "You mean it was a classic case of when rape is inevitable . . . You know the rest."

"Something like that."

"And you really expect me to get my boy to *admit* that?"

"You wouldn't have to go that far. If you thought there was any chance that Michael's assumption was correct, you could simply drop the suit."

"Rosina would never do that."

"But you're a co-plaintiff. Her suit would collapse if you withdrew."

"I daresay it would. But what do you think the tigress, deprived of her prey, would do to *me?* I'd lose my spouse, my son, and my sole means of support at one fell swoop!"

"You told me once, Eli, that the one moral principle that you had adhered to all your life was truth. That if everything else was a lie, you still had that. Isn't it worth saving no matter what the cost?"

"You're pretty free with other people's costs. You consign me to the gutter with a few noble words. And what makes you so sure that I believe that your husband's theory of what went on that dark night in my son's cubicle is correct?"

"Because you wouldn't have agreed to see me today if you didn't suspect there was something in it."

Elias chuckled. "That, I admit, is a shrewd thrust. I will also admit that we have no sure means of knowing exactly what *did* go on in that cubicle. Of course, Elihu may have lied. Scared boys often do, as you say. On the other hand he may not have. And I will also tell you frankly that, had the decision been mine alone, I would not have instituted this suit. The force behind it is solely Rosina's, but it's a terrible force."

"You could still save us. Just by admitting your doubts. Would Rosina really find that so unforgivable? Oh, Eli, I appeal to what I know is the real good at the bottom of your heart!"

"I note where you place it. No, you ask too much, Ione." He glanced at his watch. "And now, if you'll excuse me, I must be getting home. Rosina will be expecting me."

Ione arose in despair. "Will you at least think it over?"

"Ah, my dear, I think I can assure you that I shall be thinking of little else in the next few days."

But after she had gone, he did not go home. He went into the bar and had two more drinks, sitting moodily at a corner table and rejecting with a curtness most unlike him the offers of fellow members to join him. What he had not told Ione was that the father of a classmate of Elihu's at the day school the boy was now attending had called on Elias privately to explain to him why Elihu was no longer welcome at his house and why his own son would not be allowed to visit Elihu's. The classmate's father had caught the two boys playing "dirty games" together, and he refused coldly to specify what those games were. When Elias had related this later to his wife, which he had to, for Elihu was asking why he couldn't visit his pal, Rosina had become almost hysterical.

"The poor child has become hopelessly corrupted by what they did to him at Averhill! We must bend all our efforts now to saving his soul!"

"You don't think it throws any doubt on the validity of your case?"

"On *my* case! Do you mean you're not with me, Elias Castor?"

"I'm not one hundred percent sure that I am."

"You'd better make yourself sure, then," she said grimly. "Or at least button your lips on any doubt you're disloyal enough to entertain. We're in this thing together, and I shall know how to treat any defector!"

After his fourth martini Elias felt a wonderful buzzing in his head. Wonderful because it was attended with a mental view of a splendid horizon as seen from an Alpine peak. He saw himself as the apostle of truth that Ione had so eloquently invoked. He saw himself as the man he might have been had he married her. Another Michael Sayre! Why not? Of course he knew that the vision wouldn't last. Tomorrow he would be Elias Castor again, his same shabby, joking self, except with a hangover. He beckoned now to his old friend, the gently disapproving bartender, to bring him a fifth cocktail. The one thing he could do would be the one decent thing of all his days, something irradicable that no matter how far down he slipped he would never be able to forget. He would be Sydney Carton and Rosina the guillotine!

He laughed his own old laugh at the sentimental fool that he was and went to the telephone booth in the hall and dialed, with some difficulty, his lawyer's home number.

⚜ 14 ⚜

SOME MONTHS AFTER the dramatic collapse of the Castors' lawsuit and the state of Massachusetts's grudging settlement of its complaint for a nominal sum, the rehabilitated headmaster of Averhill and his much relieved wife were enjoying a restful weekend in New York as the guests of her parents. They were leisurely dressing for the small dinner the Fletchers were giving in their honor, and had treated themselves to an early cocktail.

Ione was showing a faintly uneasy curiosity about a visit her husband had paid that afternoon to Elias Castor, who, evicted from his home by Rosina, was living at one of his clubs. She had never told her husband about her one-night affair, not because she feared his jealousy but because she was ashamed of her partner.

"Well, I hadn't seen Castor since the day his case blew up," Michael explained. "And I'd never properly thanked him. After all, he gave up a lot for us."

"He righted a wrong he had done. Still, you have a point. Is he absolutely bust? Should we help him out?"

"He told me he had sold the pornographia collection he had bought with Rosina's money for a cracking sum."

"How like him!"

"And he has custody of Elihu half the year. He says the surrogate may award him an allowance out of the trust Rosina set up for the boy in the months that Elihu is with him."

Ione clapped her hands with a laugh. "You know he *is* clever. He's beaten the terrible Rosina at her own game. I guess we won't have to worry about him."

"But he told me something else. He told me that one of his reasons for killing the case was to assuage your feeling of guilt about embroiling me with Spencer. He seems to think that you wanted us to leave Averhill and that this was a way to bring it about. And that you felt responsible for the whole mess. Is that true, darling? *Did* you want to leave Averhill that much?"

Ione twisted her shoulders in discomfort. Why did this wretched thing have to come up when everything was straightened out? "Oh, maybe I did, a bit, back then. But all that's over now. These awful lawsuits have made me appreciate Averhill and what you're doing for the school. We don't know a good thing until it's about to be snatched away from us."

"But you *were* bored to death with life at school?"

"Oh, maybe a bit. But that's over, as I say."

"I knew it. And I think I've found a solution. *If* we stay at the school, which will depend on whether you think it's one. I want you to share my job, not just in theory but in fact. I want you to accept a salaried post as dean of women. The girls will soon make up half the student body, and I want you to be as much in charge of them as I am of the boys. You will have your own office and teach any course you choose. I suggest you might start with history of art. And when we get our little art gallery—I already have a couple of good pledges—you will, of course, be its curator."

"Oh, Michael!" The sudden tears stung her eyes. "You really are the perfect husband." She reached for the glass on her dresser and finished it with a gulp. "You make me feel so . . . so inadequate. I think I want another cocktail."

"Well, you're not going to have one. I don't need an alcoholic wife on my hands, like poor Donald."

Ione was too full of grateful emotion not to welcome the opportunity for an abrupt change of subject. "Speaking of whom, I suppose the great sports plaza is down the drain since his resignation from the board."

"That was only to be expected. But some of the trustees are feeling sorry about the way I've been kicked around. There's talk of raising money for a new gym. One of which even I will approve."

Ione rose now from her dressing table and moved to the door, ready to join her parents in the parlor. "Well, one thing, anyway, is clear from this whole nasty business. The Donald Spencers of this world are not going to run schools like Averhill."

Michael buttoned his dinner jacket as he joined her. "Not yet, my dear. Not yet."